ALL THE DAR

BRINA BRADY

Cover Art by Brina Brady
Editor: Anita Ford

AUTHOR'S NOTE: This book contains spanking and graphic gay sex.

DEDICATION

Thank you to all my awesome Beta Readers for helping me out until I finished my novel. Your help has been invaluable to me, and I don't know how I would have managed without your help and support. Again, thank you so much. I sincerely appreciate your help.

Grein Murray
Emma King
Sarah Mitcham
Brei-Ayn Nichole Moscato
Brenda Daulton
Ida Sue Umphers

ALL THE DARK LIES BLURB

Nineteen-year-old Nathan Neumann flees his home when an opportunity presents itself. His uncle treats him as if he were an employee, even though half the Neumann Horse Academy Ranch will be his when he turns twenty-one. He can't wait another two years.

Nathan leaves behind his life in Chadds Ford to move to London for a man he has never seen. Charles makes so many promises over six months of internet chatting. In exchange, Nathan promises to be the man's sub. One big problem, Nathan is a virgin and has only had virtual relationships. Nathan arrives in London, but Charles is nowhere in sight, only a limo driver with mysterious instructions.

Headmaster Charles Moore meets Nathan Neumann on his return flight to London. There is a strong, immediate, mutual attraction between them. Charles arrives home to find a note from his sub ending their BDSM relationship. The following morning, a limo drops Nathan at his front door. How many Charles's are there in Nathan's life?

When all the dark lies threaten to come between them, is it too late for Charles and Nathan to come clean with each other?

Age Gap. Headmaster Dom, Virgin Sub, Lies and Secrets, Light BDSM, and HEA

CHAPTER ONE

Nathan

Nathan kept the one-way ticket to London from Charles hidden under his pillow; now and then, he touched it to make sure it was still there. His abusive Uncle Lucas would have torn it up if he'd seen it and locked him in the barn for punishment. The old man treated him as if he were an employee on the lower end despite the fact that the Neumann Horse Academy Ranch would be fifty percent his when he turned twenty-one. He couldn't wait another two years.

He was up and packed at four in the morning to leave behind all his sadness along with his cruel uncle. He normally got up at this time to feed the horses and check everything before the students came for riding lessons. Everything would seem normal, so his uncle wouldn't wake up thinking something was odd. Nathan had instructed another employee to feed the horses without giving him a reason.

After he showered, he threw on a pair of tight jeans, black shirt, and a hoodie as Charles had instructed. Neither of them knew what the other really looked like. They had agreed not to send photos, leaving them surprised upon their first meeting. Nathan intentionally wore the old black boots Uncle Lucas hated, giving himself a bit of choice and freedom. He put on the braided rainbow bracelet Jacob, his best friend, had made for him. He was going to make sure everyone understood he was gay, and there wasn't a damn thing anyone could do about it. Tired and disgusted with himself for living a lie far too long, it was time to be who he was born to be.

After Nathan put his backpack on his back and picked up his old brown suitcase, he left the house through the backdoor. He turned around to see the home he had grown to hate, believing someday he'd reclaim what was rightfully his. He had been born in the bedroom on the third floor of this enormous stone house and lived here all his life. These stones had been his protective covering, tucking him inside away from the world for the years when he needed their refuge. He thanked them as he turned his back to the only home he'd known. He'd miss training horses—he knew the name of each horse—and teaching others to learn how to ride the correct way. He also would miss Alma who acted more like a mother than hired help.

When he reached the bottom of the hill, Jacob appeared from behind a tree, waiting for Nathan to say their last goodbye.

"You didn't have to meet me at this hour." It thrilled him to see Jacob, making his leaving bittersweet.

"I couldn't let you go without seeing you one last time."

"I'm glad you came."

"I know Charles will adore you when he finally sees you. I'm going to miss you terribly. It won't be the same without you."

"I'm going to miss you more than you'll ever know." Nathan pushed his tears away.

"Let me know how you make out with Charles."

"I will. You'll always be in my life, even when we're miles apart. I wish you could come with me." Nathan had known Jacob since they were both four years old. Until now, he didn't realize how much he'd miss his best friend.

"Your taxi is here." Jacob hugged him until the cab driver beeped the horn.

"I love you, Jacob. You're the brother I never had. I'll miss you so much."

"I love you, too. Don't forget we're blood brothers." He wiped his tears with the back of his hand.

The driver got out of the cab, took Nathan's suitcase and backpack, and placed them into the trunk. Nathan sat in the back and waved goodbye to his best friend through his tears as Jacob waved, his tears flowing too. Leaving his best friend was one of the hardest things he had to do.

The ride to the airport took an hour with morning traffic, the longest hour Nathan had ever experienced. When they reached the Delta Departure Terminal, the driver removed the suitcase and backpack while Nathan carried his iPad and earbuds. The driver told him to check in at the curbside booth, so he did. He handed the driver a tip, just as Charles had told him to do. So far, everything he had told him worked out exactly as he had said it would. He couldn't wait to see what Charles looked like.

Flight 103 to London would board in sixty minutes. After he went through the long forty-minute international flight security line, Nathan ran to Gate D 10. He didn't know the security line would take so long—Philadelphia Airport was a total nightmare.

Over the intercom, Nathan heard: "Delta Flight 103 to London, last call for boarding."

He continued to run, almost knocking over a little boy with a shake in his hand. By the time he reached the gate, the boarding area was empty. Out of breath, he handed his boarding pass to the ticket agent at the gate door, then she returned the ticket. He was the last passenger to board. He jogged down the long, enclosed structure to board the plane. He checked his ticket for his seat number. Seat 3A Window Seat. Charles had wanted him to enjoy the scenery instead of careless passengers bumping into him as they roamed the aisles during the long flight. He had thought of everything. The excitement to see the man, who played with him in the gay dating chat app, created butterflies in his stomach. He had made so many promises over the six months of chatting.

An older, handsome man sat in the aisle seat of his assigned row, smiling when he saw Nathan and stood up to let him into his seat. He was a tall man in good shape, dressed in a navy striped suit and pale blue shirt. Handsome in an understated way, his Spartan shoulders spoke of strength. He possessed a latent, magnificent power and stood with purpose and authority. His dark blue eyes were deep and expressive. Nathan thought he could get lost if he stared into them long enough.

Realizing he'd be stuck sitting beside this prominent businessman, Nathan regretted wearing the rainbow bracelet because the gorgeous man might say something ugly to him for being blatantly gay. He'd have to tolerate an onslaught of insults for the duration of the long flight. Nathan was so out of his element, especially dressed in jeans and wearing a hoodie over his shirt in First Class. He shouldn't think about him since he had Mr. Charles Moore waiting for him on the other side of the Atlantic Ocean. He'd be lying if he said he had the slightest doubt Charles would meet him. The problem was, he didn't have a Plan B if Charles didn't meet him at the airport.

Nathan set his backpack beside his feet, then immediately slipped his earbuds into his ears and turned up his music to block out what was happening around him, especially the takeoff. The man in the next seat tapped his shoulder, but Nathan ignored him. Shortly after the tap, the man pulled his earbuds out of his ears. Apparently, he had expected Nathan to pay attention to him.

"Hey, why did you do that?" Nathan didn't like strangers touching him without his permission. As he faced the man, he again noticed those sparkling eyes, making him want to stare at them all day and lose himself.

"Listen to the flight attendant for the safety instructions."

"Oh, thanks for letting me know." Nathan acted like a fool, displaying his flagrant ignorance. He should have read up about flying protocol. The man would think he was immature and lacked experience in traveling, which he did. Uncle Lucas had never taken him on any vacations.

"Is this your first flight?"

He's going to drive me nuts... he's too damn hot. Can someone please change seats with me?

His cock stirred inside his jeans; Nathan hoped it behaved itself.

"It is." Nathan turned off his iPad, figuring he was going to talk more.

"Are you visiting family in London?"

"Family?" Nathan shook his head. How he hated to talk about his family. Any comment pained him, bringing him to a state of hopelessness stemming from his miserable past. "No. I'm meeting my true love."

"How exciting. What does she look like?" His eyes twinkled as he spoke.

"I don't know. That's part of the thrill." Nathan wouldn't dare correct him about meeting a man, an older one at that, instead of the presumed woman.

"How old are you?" He turned his phone off and put it inside his jacket pocket.

"Nineteen." This man displayed a great deal of interest in him with no visible reason. Nathan turned his phone off, too, since the man did, and it seemed to be the thing to do. He didn't want to act as if he was stupid and uninformed. He put it inside of his backpack on the floor by his feet.

"And please don't tell me you have a one-way ticket." The concern rolled over his face.

"No point for a round-trip ticket since I plan to live there." The man made him doubt himself. His questions travelled to his heart, and all the *what-ifs* attacked him. Jacob had asked the same questions, but Nathan had put them off as Jacob hating the idea of their separation. He hadn't exactly focused on their separation when he'd accepted Charles's offer.

"Did you apply for citizenship yet?"

"No. My love will take care of that when we meet."

"I see. And do your parents know of your move to the United Kingdom?"

"By the way, I'm Nathan Neumann, and my parents died when I was twelve."

"I'm sorry to hear that. Who raised you?"

"I lived with my uncle in Chadds Ford on a horse ranch."

"The Neumann Academy Ranch? So, you're Lucas Neumann's nephew, Nathaniel?"

"Yes, but I go by Nathan, not Nathaniel." He had said too much already to the man, who could easily report his whereabouts to Uncle Lucas. He needed to stop telling strangers about his personal business. *Just be quiet or lie, you fool.*

"I'm Lawrence Wellington."

That name didn't fit this man, but he had no reason to lie, or did he? He'd never see him again after this flight, so what did he care one way or another if he had lied?

"Why are you flying to London?" Nathan asked.

"I live there."

"You don't sound like you live there." Nathan wondered if Lawrence was telling him a line of bullshit.

"I moved to London for business. What do you do for work?"

"I worked on the ranch with the horses. I gave riding lessons and took care of the horses. I had planned to go to college in the fall."

"So, you're not attending college because you're running off with the love of your life?"

"You say that like love is a bad thing." Nathan shoved his hair out of his eyes.

"It is if it takes you from preparing for life by not completing your education."

"I don't think you see the value of love at all. I can go to school anytime." This man was probably a capitalist pig, who only cared about money and nothing about love and romance. He certainly wasn't anything Nathan wanted in a man, but he was hot to look at.

"I see love as an important element in life when everything else is in place. You don't seem to have things in order for your future to remain independent."

"Independent? That's one reason I'm moving away from Chadds Ford. I want to live my life the way I want, not how others think I should be living." The man thought he was an idiot for going for love first.

"I hope you find what you're looking for. Be safe." He returned to his reading.

Nathan put his earbuds in and listened to music. After they ate lunch and dinner, they both fell asleep, and before he knew it, they'd woken up and were arriving in London.

"Thanks for talking to me," Nathan said, wishing the man wouldn't leave.

"Stay safe, Nathan." Picking up his suitcase, the man walked away heading to the coffee shop across from the luggage area.

Nathan sat and wondered why Charles wasn't at the airport like he'd promised. He looked around, but there was no one dressed in a gray suit with a green tie. He'd said that he'd hold up a sign with his name on it, so he could find him immediately. Nathan wore the clothes Charles had told him to wear so he could easily identify him at the baggage claim area. Everyone left with their luggage and their rides. He remained alone. He may have made the worst decision of his life. Going home wasn't an option because Uncle Lucas would make him suffer for running off the way he had.

This was when Plan B would have come into play if he had one. He didn't know Charles's phone number to ask where he was, nor did Charles have his either. They had never spoken on the phone, only chatted online in the gay chat room. Jacob had a bad feeling about Charles, fearing Nathan would end up sitting alone at the airport. His best friend had been right since he had been sitting alone for thirty minutes. Although, he could see Lawrence drinking his coffee, and now and then, he glanced towards him. Lawrence, at least, worried about him, but he probably didn't want to overstep.

As he caught Lawrence's attention, he thought of running to him and asking for help. He had some money but not enough to support himself in London without a job. Often, Charles had told him that he didn't want him to get a job and not to worry about money, so he didn't. No matter what, he wasn't returning to the United States. He'd make living in London work, even if he had to get a job.

CHAPTER TWO

Charles

Something about Nathan disturbed him in a way he didn't understand. The odd conversation with him on the plane seemed off. No one flies across the Atlantic Ocean to meet a person he has never seen. Somehow, his bizarre behavior displayed recklessness, putting him in physical and emotional jeopardy. Charles picked up his luggage, watching him from the corner of his eye when he found a nearby food stand and bought a cup of coffee. Nathan's face had that faraway look in it, which defied description. His smile, which reached up to his dark eyes and wrinkled them, flaunted his modesty and humility. He was as innocent as they come.

He should have given Nathan his correct name, but out of habit, he rarely did to strangers. If Nathan ran into trouble, he wouldn't have anyone to turn to in a foreign country. That young man needed to be under his watch, but he had his submissive, Hans, waiting at home. That morning, he had sent Hans a text that he was on his way. Again, no return text. This had been going on too long. He'd had no contact with him for three days. Something seemed off.

When he called him from the airport, it rang twice. Then he heard an automated message stating the number was no longer in service. He had left messages during the day, but now his phone was not in service. He had a bad feeling something was wrong with Hans. He'd find out why he was avoiding his calls and not answering his texts. His attention left Hans and returned to Nathan.

Not one damn person met Nathan after he had traveled over twelve hours on a plane. He sat there on the bench in the baggage claim area, looking at his phone as if he was waiting for it to ring, but he spoke to no one on the phone or in person. Why didn't he call his internet lover? Did he have the person's phone number or was that part of the thrill too?

In good conscience, he couldn't leave him alone in the airport with a one-way ticket and that fucking, old suitcase and backpack. Why would a young man leave the country as if he were a pauper when he was Lucas Neumann's nephew? Maybe Nathan had taken Charles for a fool. He could have made up the entire story for entertainment, but as he thought back on their conversation, he heard Nathan telling his truth from his heart. He'd never know if he was lying or not for sure.

His hesitation about leaving him alone at the airport stemmed from feeling something for him the minute he had boarded the plane. Charles sat down on a bench, making sure he could watch without Nathan seeing him. He intrigued Charles by his move across the Atlantic Ocean to meet a complete stranger and disregarding any consequences. He wondered if Nathan was the kind of young man who would seek wild sex play, and maybe like to be submissive. If he did, he'd make an adorable one for any Dominant in the lifestyle.

After thirty minutes, Nathan was still sitting alone on the same bench with his phone in his hand when a limo driver came through the doors holding a large sign with Nathan Neumann's Limo written on it. Smiling, Nathan stood up and followed the driver to the exit. Everything about Nathan brought out his need to protect and care. Obviously, living at home with his uncle hadn't worked, but his rainbow bracelet might have been the reason he left under such unusual circumstances.

Of course, Nathan wasn't meeting a woman, but he hadn't really said that in so many words. He didn't correct Charles when he had asked about the woman he had planned to meet, but his rainbow bracelet gave it away. Unfortunately, Nathan was in the process of seeking a thrill of a lifetime. Hopefully, it didn't end badly for him.

Charles followed behind him outside to the limo without being seen. He wrote down the limo's license plate number as Nathan climbed into the back. Charles had a bad feeling about him leaving, or was it a matter of him wanting Nathan for himself? He couldn't distinguish his own feelings from how the beautiful young man must have felt. Where was the limo taking him? He didn't know what to do, but his stomach contracted, twisting into a knot.

He could have prevented Nathan from getting into the limo, but he stood by and watched. Of course, it was none of his business, but he felt like he had failed him. He wanted to know more about him, especially where he was going and with who. He'd look into Nathan's whereabouts as soon as he could.

He called his driver to pick him up and made it home within an hour. His home was an enormous three-story townhouse; Nathan could have stayed with him instead of going to some unknown place with a stranger until he figured things out. Hans would have to understand that Nathan needed protection and nothing else.

As soon as Charles walked into his home, he realized something had changed. Hans didn't greet him at the door. Irritated, he went upstairs to his bedroom. On his bed, a lime green note was lying on Hans's pillow. Immediately, he picked it up and read it.

Sir,

I've decided to end our relationship. It was easier to leave when you were gone. Your lack of affection towards me left me cold and needy. That isn't who I am as a person or sub. Don't bother to look for me in the city. By the time you read this, I'll be out of the country and out of your life for good. You were a great Dom, but a lousy boyfriend.

Hans

He didn't know if he should be relieved or feel guilty. Things between them weren't working as they had in the beginning. Charles stripped off his clothes, took a long shower, and put on a pair of jeans and a T-shirt. He went behind the bar, added ice to his glass, poured a scotch, then carried his drink to the back porch, overlooking the old Weeping Willow trees. As soon as he sat in a chair and closed his eyes, his phone rang.

He picked it up, hoping it was Hans. He didn't want Hans back, but he needed closure to move on with his life.

"Hello."

"About time you got home, how was your trip?" his best friend, James, asked.

"I'm free."

"That's good. You needed closure so you can move on with your life."

"Hans left me." Charles took a long swig of his drink.

"What do you mean he's left you?"

"He returned to the Netherlands. I got home and there was a note on the bed."

"How about we meet for a drink at Jack's Pub? I missed you."

"Pick me up. I'm in no mood to drive."

"I'll be there in ten minutes."

James arrived in less than the ten minutes he'd said, and before Charles knew it, they were at Jack's. They sat in a booth and ordered scotch.

"I met someone on the plane, and now, I'm worried about him," Charles said.

"Really? Hans just left. And now you have your eye on another one?" James shook his head in disbelief.

"I said I was worried about him. I didn't say anything about fucking him."

"Why are you worried about him?" James picked up his glass.

"He flew to London to meet someone he has never seen. He waited in the airport for over thirty minutes before a limo driver picked him up."

"That sounds troubling. Was he very young?"

"Nineteen. He's Lucas Neumann's nephew." Charles and James had been raised in Chadds Ford. Everyone in Chadds Ford knew of the Neumann Riding Academy. One of the wealthiest families in the area. So, the little rich boy ran away from home at nineteen. It didn't make much sense, but there was more to the story, and he wanted to know.

"Why would Lucas allow him to do this? He's a mean fuck."

"My guess is he doesn't know."

"Maybe you should call Lucas, and he can look after him."

"Part of why he left could very well have to do with Lucas. As I recall, he's a homophobic jackass."

"Oh, you didn't mention the boy was gay." James leaned across and looked at Charles in such a way they both laughed.

"I just got the feeling he was. He wore a rainbow bracelet."

"You mean you hope he is. Anyone could wear a rainbow bracelet. That doesn't mean he's gay. Allies wear them to show their support. It's too soon for you to jump into another relationship. Hans might return when he comes to his senses."

It never crossed Charles's mind that Nathan could be an ally. No, he was gay. He didn't give any specifics of who he was meeting. He covered up informational tidbits for sure. Charles had done the same to strangers he had met.

"No, he won't be back. Things weren't working out. He wanted more than I could give him. He said I was a great Dom, but a lousy boyfriend."

"That's probably true. What are you going to do about this new one you met?"

"His name is Nathaniel, but he goes by Nathan. I wrote down the limo license plate number, so I'll go from there."

"How do you know Lucas? I don't remember you ever mentioning him."

"I bought horses from him when I lived in Chadds Ford."

"So, you've been to his ranch, and you never noticed Nathan?"

"Now that you mention it, I did see him riding a long time ago, but he was a young boy."

"So. you move here only to fall for someone from your hometown. You're a character in a Hallmark movie. I don't recognize you anymore."

"Why are you looking at me like I should know something you seem to already know?"

"Don't you remember the rumors about Lucas and the academy?"

"What rumors?"

"Lucas had his brother taken out, so he could take over the academy. Nothing has ever come of it, but it could be true."

"I hope that rumor is false."

"Since it's Saturday tomorrow, let's look for Nathan."

"Good idea. How is Tyler doing?"

"He's working at a coffee shop."

"Tyler would be a good friend for Nathan."

"Someone is getting ahead of himself."

"Can you run the limo's plates for me?"

"Sure. I'll get back to you later."

He forwarded the details to James, then they left the bar and he dropped Charles in front of his home.

As soon as he went inside, he looked around for Hans's things, but he had taken everything with him. He wondered if he had planned this move, or did he do this for another reason? He picked up his phone and called Finn, Hans's best friend in London.

"Finn, this is Charles. Did you know Hans returned to the Netherlands?"

"He told me things weren't working out, Sir. I tried to talk him into staying, but he wanted to go home."

"Was there any reason he didn't inform me of his plans?"

"He was angry at you for leaving him alone a lot. He thought you neglected him. I think he was homesick, too." His voice sounded so serious and sad that the wind stopped blowing outside.

"Do you have a contact number?"

"Yes, Sir, but he asked me not to give it to you."

"Of course, he did. Now, give me his number," Charles ordered.

"I'll send a text with it. Do you have any more questions, Sir?"

"No and thank you." He ended the call, feeling sorry for Finn losing Hans. Within a minute, Finn sent a text with Hans's new phone number.

CHAPTER THREE

Nathan

Disappointed and fearful, Nathan sat in the back of the limo without meeting Charles as he was supposed to. He promised he'd be at the airport, but he wasn't, and now he didn't know where the limo driver was taking him. Charles had broken the agreement. Why had he accepted the ride to nowhere with a limo driver who spoke little English?

"Sir, where are we going?"

"Not for me to say. He said it's a surprise."

"I don't like surprises. I want to know where the hell you're taking me."

The driver slammed the window shut so he could no longer hear Nathan, pissing him off further. Nathan pounded on the window with his fists and shouted, "Let me out of here!"

The driver never answered and continued driving as if Nathan hadn't been pounding on the window. Things were turning out badly. He shouldn't have trusted Charles. He didn't even know his phone number.

The limo stopped at a hotel. The driver got out, opened the door for Nathan and said, "You are to check in here. Just say your name. Charles paid for everything. He will meet you in the morning. He had an emergency today."

"Are you sure he's coming tomorrow?" Nathan feared the limo driver was lying to him.

By then the driver had carried Nathan's things into the hotel and called a bellman to take them.

"Check in there," he pointed to the check-in counter.

Nathan walked over to the counter and told them his name. They gave him a key without him paying. So, the driver was right, Charles had paid for the suite. The bellman directed him to follow him to the elevator. The bellman ran the card, unlocking the door, then he put his suitcase and backpack on a bench.

"Will you be needing anything else, sir?"

"No. And thank you." Nathan handed him a tip.

Once the bellman left the room, he locked the door and checked out the room. He had no complaints about size and comforts in here. It had one king-size bed, a TV, Wi-Fi, and a little kitchen area. He looked inside the refrigerator and pulled out a bottle of Amstel Light Beer. Someone had stacked it with Amstel Light Beer and Coke. Charles had asked him what his favorite drinks were, alcoholic and non-alcoholic. The man had gotten that part right, but not meeting him at the airport was a double-edged hurt, though, because he had adored Charles. His deep feelings for him faded as he realized he was alone in a foreign country. Nor did he trust Charles the same way he had.

He sat up on the bed and turned on the TV with the remote. What was he supposed to do here without Charles? The limo driver didn't seem trustworthy because he had refused to answer many of his questions. However, he could've dropped him at the bottom of the River Thames. The thought shook his insides as he imagined what could have happened by accepting a ride from someone he didn't know to go to an unknown area.

He took his phone out and called Jacob.

"Hey, are you okay?" Jacob asked.

"I'm fucked. Charles didn't meet me at the airport. He sent a limo driver. Thirty fucking minutes later. He took me to a paid hotel room and said Charles will see me in the morning. I don't know what to think."

"Come home. Use the credit card I gave you. That's what it's for. Please don't stay there alone. He broke his promise. What else will he break?"

"I met this hot guy on the plane. He moved here for work, but maybe I should see if I could find him. I only have his name, Lawrence Wellington."

"You know even less about Lawrence than Charles. Nothing good can happen there. Charles lied. He's a damn predator. What if your uncle set up Charles to catch you in a gay relationship?"

"I never thought of that. Lawrence said he knew my uncle. He was asking a lot of questions about me. I never told him who exactly I was going to meet. He thinks I was going to meet a woman."

"That's really odd you would sit beside a man who happens to know your uncle, don't you think?" Jacob spoke with a concerned tone in his voice, one he had known from the past.

"I guess so. I hadn't thought it was odd. If I don't see him tomorrow, then I'll think of something else. I wish you would come out to see me. We could travel together if Charles doesn't work out."

"I'll think about it. I have a job and I'd have to get some time off."

"I'll call you tomorrow and let you know what's going on."

"Stay safe."

"I will." Nathan ended the call, feeling lonelier than ever. Here he was all alone in a hotel room when he thought today was the day he'd meet Charles. What if Charles had come to the airport and didn't like what he saw? That's what must have happened, then he dumped him here for the night. He wasn't about to stay in this room like a fool. He was in London for the first time and decided to enjoy the evening. He might never get another chance to enjoy a different slice of life other than his pathetic life at the academy with Uncle Lucas.

After he showered, he changed into clean clothes. He took the elevator to the third floor and found the restaurant. The server seated him at a table with a menu. He ordered a beer and said he would order after he read the menu. He signed into the online chat room, planning to message Charles, but he'd closed his account this morning. That could mean two things: he stopped looking for another man, or he ended all communication with Nathan. Disappointment spiraled through him as reality hit. He questioned his own decision to leave his home. Why didn't he move to another state? He thought Charles would take care of him. And what he thought would be his first-time having sex never happened, he still was a virgin. A young woman with a flawless, bronzed complexion sat at a table across from him and smiled. He returned the smile. She was waif-thin with luscious lips. Her red nails and makeup accented her pretty dress. She was picture perfect.

"Hey, why don't you join me, sugar?" she asked.

"Thank you." He was tired of being alone, as he had been most of his life, but he had Jacob, who he terribly missed. It couldn't hurt any, and he could use a friend here.

He got up, took his menu, and sat across from her. "My name is Nathan Neumann."

"I'm Willow Starr. You don't sound like you're from here." She shot him another friendly smile.

The server brought Willow a menu.

"I flew in from Philadelphia today, but you sound like you're from here."

"Yes. Why are you alone?"

"I was supposed to meet someone, but they didn't show up at the airport. They set me up here and said they'll meet me tomorrow."

"That doesn't sound very good. Why didn't you call to find out why?"

"I don't know the number." He waited for her to say something derogatory to him for being so stupid.

The server returned; they both ordered a steak platter.

"Would you like to go to a party?"

"What kind of party?"

"A friend of mine is having a party upstairs in a suite. It's just young college people having a good time. You can go with me."

"Thanks for inviting me. I had nothing to do by myself."

"Are you going to stay in London or return to Philadelphia if you guys don't meet up tomorrow?"

The server brought their dinners.

"I'll see how it goes and then decide."

"Do you need a job?"

"I'll probably need one."

"What skills do you have?"

"I'm a riding instructor, plus I trained horses."

"I know of a riding school nearby. I'll check it out for you. Can I have your number?"

Nathan pushed his Neumann Riding Academy business card across the table.

"Here's my number if you just need to talk." She handed him a hot pink card with her phone number on it. He looked closer, noticing she was an escort. People paid to be with her.

"Thank you for helping me," Nathan said.

"Yes, you read right. I sell my body. But I'm not asking you to pay to be with me. I have friends too, plus you like men."

"How do you know I prefer men?" Her discernment of his gender preference startled him. Now, he had to wonder if others could tell, but no one at home had said anything.

"You didn't hit on me right away like most men, and you're wearing a rainbow bracelet. I love gay men. They make the best friends because they care about me, not getting sexual favors for free from me."

"I don't judge anyone, and I wish people wouldn't judge me. I like you because you're okay with me being gay. I don't discuss it with anyone. For some strange reason, I feel safe with you."

"Then we'll make good friends. Are you staying in London?"

"For tonight, I am. But I'm supposed to meet Charles tomorrow if he shows up."

"Look, if he doesn't, you can hang out at my place until you decide what you want to do. I live alone."

"Thanks. That's generous of you. I'll call you if I'm stood up again. I'm giving him until noon, then whatever we had is over. He's a liar and a con."

"Did he pay for your ticket?"

"Yes."

"Sounds like he's making an investment in you, but you need to be careful. There are all kinds of crazy people, who live to hurt others. I wouldn't want anything to happen to you."

After they finished dinner, Willow's phone rang. She answered it, then turned to him.

"They changed the location of the party. It's near here. We can walk."

"That sounds okay with me."

Once they reached the apartment, many male college students, and a few females, who were dressed to work on the men for fast cash, filled the room.

"Let me get you a drink," she said.

As soon as Willow left, he shrugged off an uncomfortable feeling that something was amiss, especially those few guys staring at him. They knew he didn't belong here, so he might as well leave. Before she returned, he was out the door and walking back to the hotel. He saw a shortcut between two buildings, curtailing the distance considerably, so he took it. Then he wished he hadn't. Two men followed him into the dark alley. Nathan picked up his pace and tried to get to the other side before they reached him. He started running, but the two men ran faster than he did and caught up with him. He recognized one from the party, but he didn't remember seeing the other one there.

The larger one shoved him against the building. Without saying anything, they punched him in his face, stomach, and anywhere they could reach. Nathan fought back kicking and punching, but with two against one, he was no match. One pulled out a knife, sliced his rainbow bracelet from his wrist, then the asshole stomped on it.

"Die, you little queer."

"Go back where you came from. We don't want your kind here," the other one said.

He thought this would be the end of him, when he'd seen the knife move towards his face. Nathan kicked the guy with the knife away, making him land on the ground. He got lucky in his time of need.

"Stop! Just stop! Help," Nathan shouted louder. Then another two men ran to them. They fought the two guys who hurt him. They were shouting at them to stop, and both landed on top of a trashcan. He wondered who these two men were.

"Run," one of them shouted to Nathan.

He picked up his sliced bracelet, stuffed it into his pocket, and jogged to the other end of the alley, where the sidewalks and streets were busy. He was safe from any further threats. All he wanted was to reach his hotel room. He'd never make that mistake again. He ran all the way to the hotel and took the elevator to his room. He showered to clean the blood away, then threw himself on the bed, and called his best friend.

"Hey, how is it going?" Jacob asked.

"Not good. I got jumped in an alley."

"Are you okay?"

"Just bruised a little, and everything hurts. Two men saved me. They pulled the two guys off me and I ran back to the hotel."

"Where were you going?"

"I met this girl, and we went to a party. As soon as we got there, I had a funny feeling, so I left. They followed me from the party. They went after me because I'm gay."

"If you went to the party with a girl, why would they think you're gay?"

"I wore your rainbow bracelet, and she told me she has lots of gay friends. So, maybe that was it. The fucker sliced the bracelet you made. I wanted to kill him, but they caught me off guard."

"Don't worry. I'll make you another one and send it to you when you have an address. Your uncle hasn't said anything to anyone."

"He never cared about me."

"It might be worse than not caring. He might be part of this mess you're in. I wish you'd come home. Stay with me. You're not safe over there. No one knows you."

"I'll think about it. I want to see what happens tomorrow. I have a feeling I'll never meet Charles."

"He was catfishing you. He could be a woman for all we know."

"I hope you're wrong, but something tells me Charles made a fool out of me."

"Just come home, please."

"I'll call you after I meet Charles."

"Don't forget, or I'll call you."

CHAPTER FOUR

Charles

The morning brought the reality he once again lived in a large empty home alone. All his relationships lasted no longer than a year before they left him. He'd go to the club tonight and find a boy to play with, then take him home for the night. He didn't want to deal with his mistakes with Hans, nor was he ready to talk to him.

The major problem was he had collared boys who played well, but he didn't have strong feelings towards any of them. He strictly picked a partner based on their level of obedience to him, and Hans fit the bill. Did he love Hans? No. He cared about him on many levels but felt like he'd failed him for not loving him the way he needed. Hans and James were right about him being a lousy boyfriend and lover. He needed to stop collaring boys unless he loved them enough. A Dom didn't need to love his sub, but he wanted more than a sub. He'd be very cautious with collaring another sub and play with different ones until he felt something. No more sex based contracts. He wanted someone to love and care for.

His thoughts turned to Nathan. Right off, he'd felt something with him, and he didn't act on it, but he had thought Hans was his sub and lover. Charles picked up his phone and sent James another message to see if he'd found any information on the limo at the airport. He made himself some coffee to go with his quick breakfast of toast and butter. Hans used to make the meals when they didn't go out. He'd miss his cooking and his conversation in the morning. The boy was a perfect sub; any Dom would love him to pieces. He was picture perfect at all times, but Charles couldn't love him the way he'd wanted.

His phone rang, and he answered, expecting Hans to return his calls and messages with a few dozen apologies. "Hello."

"The limo comes from Shaylen's Limo Service in London. I called and asked about the driver who went to the airport to pick up Nathan Neumann. He didn't want to give much out, but I told him there was an investigation into the disappearance of Nathan. He said it was paid in cash and left no information. However, he said he dropped Nathan off at Claridge's Hotel. So, you can check out the hotel."

"Thanks." Charles immediately called Claridge's and asked for Nathan Neumann's room. They connected his call to his room, but no one picked it up.

The hotel operator interrupted after the ringing stopped. "Do you want to leave a message?"

"Please give him my number and ask him to call as soon as he can. Tell him it belongs to the man who sat beside him on the plane." He left his phone number with the operator.

He returned to the kitchen and noticed Hans had left his special mug. Charles picked it up when he saw left over gold liquid and smelled it. The last thing he'd drunk had been straight scotch, something he never had, or at least not in front of him. Hans didn't drink any alcohol by his choice, and Charles respected him for it. Every morning, Hans drank his tea in this mug. He wondered why he didn't take it with him, but it would remind him of something he'd left behind. Charles had given it to him the day he collared him. It had writing on it stating Hans belonged to Charles. Apparently, Hans no longer wanted to belong to Charles since he'd left without notice.

Again, Charles felt guilty for not working hard enough to meet Hans's needs. Playing in the dungeon was easy for him. He thrived as a Dom, but when he ended a scene, a part of him disappeared. Every young man he had collared over the years had the same complaint. He noticed no other Dom having this issue. All his subs left him—some even found another Dom while they were with him.

When the doorbell rang, Charles felt a rush of panic run through him when he thought Hans had returned and changed his mind. He answered the door without looking through the peephole first, as he routinely had done. He couldn't believe who stood on his porch with his old suitcase and backpack.

"Nathan? Come in." He hadn't given him his address, but here he was. This little rich boy must have connections to locate his home with only the phone number he'd left with the hotel. As he looked at Nathan closer, he noticed bruises covered his sweet face.

"The limo driver said Charles Moore lives here, and he's expecting me. I don't understand why you answered his door."

"What happened to your face?" Charles ignored the comment. Pity for the boy increased as he studied the bruises on his arms and face. He looked like a damaged angel. Did this internet man do this to him or maybe some of his hires?

"Some guys didn't like me being..."

Charles took his arm, pulling him inside. "Please come in, so I can help you take care of your bruises." The limo had left before Charles had seen it, but Nathan had said the limo driver dropped him off here, and he believed him.

Charles took Nathan's suitcase and backpack, then set them down in the hallway. He led him to the kitchen.

"Are you staying here until Charles comes home?"

"Sit down," he pointed to the kitchen chair. "We'll talk in a minute. I need to check your bruises."

"I'll be okay. Just a few punches here and there."

Charles got a warm washcloth and put some mild soap on it. He washed his bruises, then rinsed them with another cloth. "Does it hurt?"

"Just a little."

"Are you bruised anywhere else?"

"Just my arms. Two guys came out of nowhere and broke it up."

"I'd like to take you to a doctor to make sure everything is okay."

"I'll be fine. So, are you going to explain where Charles is?"

Charles sat down facing Nathan.

"First, Charles Moore is my actual name, but I'm not the Charles Moore you're looking for. When I travel, I never give my real name for good reason."

"So, have you been the one writing to me in the chat room? Did you pay for my ticket?"

"I never wrote to you in any chat room, nor did I pay for your ticket. I don't understand exactly how you got here, but I'm pleased to see you again. I left a message at your hotel."

"I didn't get any messages."

"Did the limo driver ask you where you wanted to go?"

"No. He picked me up at the hotel this morning, drove for two hours around the city, then dropped me off here. He said Charles Moore is ready for me and lives here. As soon as I got out of the limo with my things, he drove away."

"He's partially correct. I'm Charles Moore, and I live here. I might not have been expecting you, but I'm delighted to see you again." Charles shot him a big welcoming smile.

"Do you think the internet man used your name?"

"He must have. You said you were chatting with Charles Moore, but I'm not that Charles. But I'd like to help you though, so you don't have to return home."

"Why would you want to?"

"Because I feel like I've been called to watch over you, and I like you."

"I didn't think you did."

"Why would you think that?"

"I dressed like a bum compared to you, and I sounded stupid meeting someone I never saw before."

"I don't think you're stupid at all. You let your guard down and took a risk by coming here. I know Chadds Ford isn't the best place for a gay boy. I mean, young man."

"No one knows back there. Except my best friend. I had to get away from my uncle. He'd kill me if he ever found out."

"You're safe being gay in my home. I'm gay too, but I'm not out at my job."

"You're gay? I'd never guess that. I was worried you'd call me names for wearing my rainbow bracelet."

Charles nodded his head in disbelief. "You know what I want to say to you?"

"What?"

"I like you, Nathan, and I'm glad you landed in my home, but I'm worried about someone using my name in gay chat rooms."

"So, you really never wrote to me in a chat room?" Nathan looked disappointed.

"No. I don't go to chat rooms. I go to a special club to meet men."

"Do you have a boyfriend?"

"Not anymore. He left while I was in Philadelphia."

"I'm sorry that happened. I guess I should leave since the Charles Moore from the chat room is not you."

"Let's talk about that, but first, would you like some tea?"

"No, thank you. I don't drink tea."

"How about a glass of orange juice?"

"Yes, thanks."

Charles poured juice into a tall glass, setting it on the table, then poured himself more coffee.

"I'd like you to stay with me. I have plenty of guest rooms. I want to help you settle in here before you take off." He sat down across from Nathan.

"I have a place to stay if I need it. I met this girl last night, and she said I could hang out with her."

"So, you just met her?"

"Yes. We went to a party, but I left because I didn't feel comfortable."

"Stay with me. Let me help you. I need to do that."

The doorbell rang.

"Should I leave through the back door?"

"No. You're not leaving until we finish our conversation. I'm not ashamed of you if that's what you're thinking. Stay put."

Nathan smiled and took a sip of his juice.

CHAPTER FIVE

Nathan

While Nathan waited for Charles to return from answering the front door, he noticed a green board nailed to the wall with five written house rules on it. He could read them from sitting in the chair. The white chalk letters were large and readable.

Rule One: Obey me the first time.

Rule Two: No lying or any form of dishonest behavior.

Rule Three: Do not withhold any information from Master Charles.

Rule Four: Check in while out of the house.

Rule Five: Master Charles has the final say in all matters.

Master Charles...

So, Charles was Master Charles of something. Who were those rules for? He wondered, if he stayed, would Charles expect him to follow those rules, too? He'd better ask him before he agreed to stay. There was no question, Charles made his cock harden at the very sight of him and the sound of his voice, but he didn't understand why those house rules also made him tingle in all the right places. Some people had rules for guests. Somehow, everything Charles had done made him feel awakened. Why couldn't this Charles be the Charles in the chat? This Charles certainly had enough money to purchase him a one-way ticket, but why would he communicate only in a gay chat?

He'd also ask about the club where he met men. He said a special club, which could be as simple as going to a gay club. He had never been to one near his home for fear word would get back to Uncle Lucas. The man frightened Nathan on many levels, so he avoided him as much as possible. However, he was forced to have dinner with him every night. That's when he would turn Nathan into an emotional wreck by his constant criticisms and put-downs. This entire mess was disappointing and confusing, but it was nothing compared to living a lie with his uncle.

Nathan had read about relationships with rules in fiction books. Sex on demand was the basic theme and discipline for inappropriate behavior. He enjoyed reading about a man submitting to another man, and the thought of Charles spanking him turned him on. He also liked the idea of having a permanent sexual partner. Is this what Charles wanted?

At nineteen years old, he was still a damn virgin. Jacob always wanted to try out sex with him, but Nathan had declined. He loved him, but not in that way. He had decided a long time ago, he'd never hurt Jacob or risk their friendship. They had long discussions about having sex with each other for experimentation and added experience, but Jacob finally agreed it might cause problems in their perfect friendship. However, both remained without any experience, other than what they'd shared from their reading or watching gay videos online.

When Charles returned, there were two others following behind him. One man was older, like Charles, and the other was around his age. The older man was the same height as Charles, and he had a few streaks of gray in his dark hair. The younger one had brown, curly hair and soft brown eyes. He was much smaller than the older man.

"Nathan, these are my friends, James and his sub, Tyler. Believe it or not, they came here to help me find you."

"Me?" Nathan embarrassed easily and could feel his face warming into a blush, advertising his awkwardness.

"James helped me find where you were staying and thought they might be able to help me look for you if you didn't call."

"Hi, James and Tyler," Nathan said.

James looked at Charles as if he had a question about Nathan.

"He got jumped last night."

"Are you okay?" James asked.

"Yes, just some bruises."

"Since you found him, do you guys want to meet us at the club later on?"

"I'm not sure Nathan wants or is ready to go there," Charles said.

"I want to go," Nathan said.

"Then we'll go." Charles smiled as if he were happy to take him; and for all he knew, maybe he was. He should give Charles a go, but those rules needed explaining.

"I need to discuss something with you first," James said.

"Let's go to the back porch, then these two can get to know each other." Charles ran his hand over Nathan's hair. "I'll be right outside if you need me."

"Thanks," Nathan said.

"Are you Charles's new sub?" Tyler asked.

"No. I'm nothing to him."

"I'm a sub. James is my Dom. He takes care of me, and in exchange, I follow his rules and please him in any way he wants. Do you know anything about BDSM relationships?"

"Only from Anne Rice's books."

"Those books are great."

"Did you know his last sub?" Nathan changed the subject as he became uncomfortable with his display of ignorance once again. He was brilliant in high school, but in the real world, he was an idiot, thanks to Uncle Lucas.

"Yes. Hans. He left Charles and returned to the Netherlands. He was one of my friends."

"Was he cute?" Nathan asked.

"Very. Blond hair, blue eyes, and on the small side. He was a nice guy, and I'm going to miss him. Are you interested in Charles?"

"I guess he's sad about Hans leaving." Nathan didn't feel safe telling Tyler his feelings for Charles, and he was still confused about the internet man even after he'd met *this* Charles Moore. Still, he wondered if he *was* the one he'd talked to in the chat room.

"He gets a new one every year and they all leave him because he doesn't love them. Don't tell him I said that, but you might be the one he keeps if you go for him."

"What you say to me is between us."

"That's good. Would you like to know more about the lifestyle?"

"I do have one question." Nathan pointed to the rules on the green board. "Were these rules for Hans?"

"Those were his house rules. Charles had rules for him in the playroom and other situations."

"Does he have a playroom in this house?" He was shocked there might be one in the house and didn't know if he should be open to it or run. The dungeons or playrooms he had seen in online videos looked like scary-torture chambers. Internet Charles had one, but it didn't look scary.

"Yes, many Doms have a room to play in."

"What's in there?"

"If you ask Charles, I'm sure he'll let you see it. He'll explain the spanking implements and the different furniture pieces."

"Does James spank you?" Nathan wished he had filtered his question. His ignorance and interests were right out there.

"Sure he does. Almost all Doms spank their subs, but it only happens if both agree. You could read up on it for answers. There are things I can't explain, or I might say wrong. Did Charles tell you he was a Dom?"

"No. All he said was he finds young men in a special club. He didn't go into detail, but maybe he will if I ask. He seems friendly."

"Where did you meet him?"

"He sat beside me on the plane. We talked a lot. I told him about the person I was going to meet, but I never mentioned he was a man. I didn't know he was gay too."

"So, James said you never saw the person or talked to him on the phone. Is that true?"

"Yes, it's true."

"Charles was worried about you. That's how it begins. A Dom worries about the boy he cares for and is always wanting to help him. Before you know it, he's your Dom, and you're his sub. It's fun. Tonight, I could bring you a beginner's book to read, if you'd like."

"Is it fiction or non-fiction?" Nathan couldn't imagine a non-fiction book on the topic.

"Non-fiction."

Charles and James entered the kitchen, looking happier than when they'd left. They must have had a productive conversation.

"We'll see you guys tonight," James said.

They said their goodbyes and left.

"Can I ask you something?" Nathan asked.

"Anything within reason."

"Those rules over there." Nathan pointed to them. "Are they for all your guests or just special ones?"

"Those rules were for my last sub, Hans. He is no longer with me."

"So, if I decide to stay here until I figure out what I want to do, will I have to follow those rules?"

"Let's talk about each rule and see how you feel about them. Are you okay with that?"

"I can *talk* about them." Nathan emphasized the word talk.

"The first rule applies to a Dom/sub relationship. For example, if I asked you to do something for me, you'd do it, but we don't have that type of relationship."

"Does that mean we never will?"

"That's up to you, but you need to understand the expectations to become my sub. We aren't anywhere near that. We just met."

"So, I'm too stupid to be your sub?"

"When and if I make you my sub, your first rule will be never to speak badly of yourself. You're not stupid. I like you. Don't put yourself down over a lifestyle you haven't been acquainted with. Read the next rule to me."

"No lying or any form of dishonest behavior."

"Whether you're my houseguest, friend, sub, or acquaintance, do you agree to be honest with me?"

"I'm honest, and that rule won't be a problem for me, but you lied to me. You told me your name was Lawrence Wellington, but you're Charles Moore."

"I'm sorry I lied to you. For the purpose of keeping my lifestyle distanced from my work life, I never use my real name. However, you have a good point. I promise I'll be honest with you. I'll answer any question you have with complete honesty."

"So, then you'll follow rule two also?"

"Yes, I promise you."

"Okay, then we agree to rule two."

"Who is the Dom here? You or me?"

"Not me."

"Read rule three to me."

"Do not withhold any information from *Master* Charles." Nathan emphasized the word Master. He'd called no one master before. It sounded so medieval, like it belonged in a history book or Anne Rice's novels.

"Do you have a problem with the word master?"

"It doesn't sound normal to use that title in today's world."

"You won't be calling me Master Charles since I'm not your Dom. Tell me, would you be okay with telling me things about yourself, so we can get to know each other better?"

"I'm an open book to you. I have nothing to hide or protect by omitting anything."

"So do we agree with rule three without the title Master?"

"Yes, I agree. But are you saying I can never call you Master Charles?"

"The word never is not in my dictionary. If you're interested, I'd like to get to know you and introduce you to my lifestyle."

"I'd like to see what it's all about."

"I like your open mind. Read rule four."

"Check in while out of the house."

"Would that be okay if you let me know when you're leaving, so I don't worry about you?"

"I guess I could, but I have nowhere to go."

"You'll have lots of places to visit, and I bet Tyler will ask you to do things with him and some of the other subs."

"But I'm not a sub."

"Not a problem. They'll like you, anyway. I like you."

"I like you too unless you turn into a crazy man."

"That won't happen. Read rule five."

"Master Charles has the final say in all matters."

"This rule doesn't apply to you because I don't have the final say in all matters, especially pertaining to you."

"Okay then."

"You look disappointed."

"Your last boyfriend and you agreed to rule five, but you're right, we're nothing to each other."

"I never said we were nothing. We're learning about each other. Where it goes is up to you. Right now isn't forever. Things change. We'll see how it goes. Let's look at the room you'll be sleeping in."

Nathan popped out of his chair with a great deal of excitement about sleeping in Charles's home. He wondered if they would ever sleep together. He ought to mention he'd never had sex before. It didn't seem to be the right time since there was no mention of sex, and Charles hadn't made any sexual overtures towards him either.

"Ever since you stepped on the plane, you touch me in a way most men don't. It was effortless to care about you. I didn't have to try because it was instant. I didn't understand it, but you're very handsome."

"I thought you were too good for me. You looked like you had everything together in your life."

"No one is too good for you. You'll learn to love who you are. Maybe your uncle didn't instill confidence into you when you were growing up. And someday, we need to talk about him."

"Have you ever met him in person?"

"I bought horses from him years ago. I saw a young boy riding a horse, and when I asked about you, he told me you were his nephew."

"Why did you ask about me?" Nathan asked.

"I thought you rode your horse like a professional, yet you were so young at the time. Your riding impressed me."

"Thank you. Did you live near Chadds Ford?"

"Yes. I was raised in Chadds Ford too. I got married there." He stopped at the door. "This is your room. You can do what you want in here without worrying about me walking in. I'll always knock first. Just don't smoke in my home."

"I don't smoke." Nathan couldn't get it out of his mind Charles had been married in the town he was raised in.

"That's good news." He opened the door. "You can put your clothes in the drawers and closet. The TV works. The food in my home is for you. Eat and drink what you like."

"Thank you. I didn't tell you this, but I'm happy you answered the door. I'm also thrilled you asked me to stay."

"I'm glad you knocked on my door. Now I want you to feel at home. I need to check on some things at work, so I'll be back in a few hours. Then we'll eat dinner and meet James and Tyler."

"Sounds good."

"Let me know if you need anything. The room has a bathroom attached so you'll have privacy."

"Thanks."

CHAPTER SIX

Charles

Charles took his sports car to visit Logan, his friend who worked for the police department. He originally asked to see Logan as soon as he had heard Nathan's story and wanted to locate him, but once he ended up at his door with another story, he needed his friend to figure out what he should do. Someone was setting him up.

"How was your trip?" Logan asked as they walked to the living room.

"It was stressful, but it's over. I closed up all the loose ends. So, there is nothing there for me."

"Good. Can you go to dinner tonight?" Logan made each of them a scotch on the rocks, regardless of the early hour in the day.

"I have other plans, but I'll take a raincheck." He sipped his drink.

"You said on the phone you have a problem you wanted me to look into."

"Someone is using my name in a gay chat room. He not only used my name to flirt but sent a young man to my home. This internet person communicated with a young man named Nathan Neumann and promised him the world. He even sent him a ticket to London from the United States. Somehow, this young man sat beside me on the plane."

"That's some crazy story. So, someone in London used your name and convinced this young man to fly to London to meet up?"

"Nathan is upset. This man lied to him. He left home because things weren't going well. He's from the same town as I am, but I don't understand why this man used my name."

"How did Nathan know where you lived?"

"This morning, a limo driver dropped him off. He thought he was at the home of the person he chatted with on the internet. I let him in because I knew a little about him from when we had chatted on the plane. He's only nineteen."

"We need to find the internet man who is using your name and why. Are you going to send Nathan back home?"

"No. Right now, he's figuring out what he wants to do."

"I'd like to meet with him. I need more information about the chat room."

"I'll ask him if he'll speak to you. Last night, two guys jumped him, and his face was covered in bruises. He's resting at my place."

"He could get lost at your home. This sounds like it could be a setup, but I'm not sure which one of you is being set up. We'll sort this out."

"Someone wants to out me. But why?"

"The only thing that comes to mind is the religious boarding school you teach at."

"They promoted me to headmaster."

"Congratulations. Do you have any enemies there?"

"I have a few who dislike me because of my promotion. There's always competition for the top position."

"Make me a list of those who were competing for your current position."

"It has to be someone who knew my hometown and traveling schedule. I don't remember going into detail about it to anyone at school."

"That is where I want to begin, and they don't need you to tell them where you're from. I never liked you working there because of their stand on gay people. Once they find out or can prove you're gay, then they will get rid of you."

"That might be a possibility."

"Keeping Nathan at your home doesn't help, but at this point, live your life as you've been doing. This internet man can't be allowed to use your name and send a young man to your home. I can't imagine how he set this up. He befriends a gay boy from your hometown, invites him to visit, and the boy ends up sitting beside you, then a limo drives him to your home. Is there any way Nathan is part of this?"

"No. If anyone isn't trustworthy, it's me. I didn't tell him my correct name when we met."

"And he did? You know this how?"

"He said that's what his name was and mentioned the ranch where he lived."

"Have you seen any documentation on him?"

"No. Should I?"

"I would've thought you'd have checked his driver's license before inviting him to stay at your home."

"No, I didn't. I trust him."

"That is so unlike you. I'll interview him if he's okay with it."

"I'll talk to him and see how he feels."

"What does Hans have to say about him?"

"He returned to the Netherlands without any notice while I was in the States. He left me a note on my bed."

"I didn't see that coming. He seemed to worship you. What happened?"

"Not any one thing. He wanted something I couldn't give him."

"Your life is complicated."

"Thanks for helping. I need to get back home."

All he could think about was Nathan. There was no way Nathan could be involved with outing him. He trusted Nathan, but he needed to know more about him. More than he knew about him at the moment. To think, his heart was all wrapped up with Nathan. He was acting like a schoolboy with a crush. This feeling he had was deeper than a crush, and it made no sense. He needed a sub, not some boy off a horse ranch from Pennsylvania. Here he was in London and could find a sub at the club, and he'd fallen for someone from his hometown, who wasn't sub material that he knew of. All of this was based on Nathan telling him the truth, but his gut told him Nathan was innocent and had fallen victim to the internet man.

When he walked into the house, he saw Nathan sitting on the couch with a book in his hand. Charles was impressed he read instead of watching TV.

"How are you feeling, Nathan?"

"Much better. Your house is filled with so many rooms."

"Yes, it is. I'd like to talk to you about something confidential."

"I don't know anyone to tell and of course, I'd keep whatever you say to myself."

"Good. I am a headmaster at a private religious school. This is why I keep my lifestyle and gender preference to myself and close friends. It's important no one at my work finds out. I have a friend who would like to talk to you about the chat room. Someone used my name and address to lure you here with me."

"I can leave so you won't have to worry about being outed by anyone. I can call the girl I met."

"The last thing I want is for you to leave. Please understand I like you and want the best outcome for you. I'm telling you this because we need to find out who lured you here using my name."

"I don't want to cause any trouble."

"You're no trouble at all. Tell me about your life back home. I'd like to know you better."

"I worked a lot and my friend Jacob and I used to go riding for hours. We went hiking and bowling. We didn't have a social life."

"Is Jacob your boyfriend?"

"Oh no. We've known each other since kindergarten. We're best friends."

"Any boyfriends?"

"Only the Charles I was chatting with. He told me he loved me and wanted to start a new life with me. He convinced me to agree not to send pictures, and he refused to give me his phone number. I should have figured out he was a con man because no one would love me the way he said he did and not show up. I mean, I had nothing going on, and he just said loving things to me. I believed him." Nathan bowed his head as if he were ashamed.

"Have you been with a man?"

"No. Not yet. I was hoping Charles and I would be together last night. I was really looking forward to it. He talked about it each time we chatted."

"I think we'll take things slowly, and please don't see that as me not liking you enough. That's not the problem here. You need to feel safe with me."

"You don't have to baby me. I want a life with a man, and I'm willing to take a chance."

"Tonight, you will enter my world, and you can see what I'm about and what I want. Ask me anything you want."

"Do you think Hans will come back?"

"He left for good. Things weren't working between us."

"But what if he came back? Would you take him back?"

"No. What are you reading?"

"Anne Rice's Beauty's Punishment. I love all her books."

"She's a talented author for sure. I've read her books too. How far are you into this book?"

"I'm at the beginning, but I've read it twice before. I love it."

"That's good to know. Tonight, at the club, you'll see how leather men play with their subs."

"Will I be your sub for the night?"

"No, I don't think so. We'll just look around at what others are doing, and if you want to try something, we'll see."

"Thanks for treating me like an adult." Nathan smiled, which was rare.

"For tonight you'll need a safeword. It's a word you can say, and I'll know you've had enough. Some use red, others use something of their choosing. What is a word you'll remember?

"Red, Sir."

"If you feel uncomfortable tonight, use your safeword." The boy called him Sir. He hadn't told him to address him as Sir. This was moving along faster than he'd ever imagined.

"Thank you, Sir."

Charles grew excited when Nathan showed interest in the club activities. He imagined pushing Nathan's boundaries in his playroom and at the club. Eventually, Charles would need a sub, whether it be him or someone else. He hoped Nathan would grow to love the lifestyle, but for now, he'd begin with kissing when the time was right.

"I'm going to make you dinner but tell me if there is anything you don't like."

"I like everything unless it's too hot."

"You don't like spicy food?"

"I like some spices, but if it's red hot, I can't eat it."

"Do you like fish and chips?"

"Yes, I can help you."

"Let's wash our hands and start cooking."

They stood by the counter, and Charles handed Nathan eggs to beat in a bowl while he got the coating made up. He was quiet for the most part, unlike Hans, who chatted constantly. He wondered what Nathan was thinking, and whether he believed he wasn't the Charles who chatted dirty things to him. Even though the two of them met on the plane, he reacted to Charles as if he had known him for a while.

"Did you cook at home?"

"My uncle hired a woman who cooked and cleaned. Basically, she did everything in the house. Alma was really good to me."

"So, you didn't cook at all?"

"Alma taught me how. She said I needed to live on my own someday, and she let me help her many times."

"Did you tell Alma you were leaving?"

"No. I was afraid she'd feel it was her duty to tell my uncle."

"I hope at some point you contact her and let her know you're safe."

"I will. Can I fry the fish?"

When dinner was ready, Charles seated Nathan on his right side at the long rectangular table covered with a lace tablecloth in the dining room. The furniture was dark, but the padding on the chairs was blue. Colorful art framed two walls.

"You did an excellent job."

"Thanks."

CHAPTER SEVEN

Nathan

After dinner, Nathan changed into jeans and a clean shirt. Charles knocked on his door.

"Come in," Nathan said, putting his book down on the bed.

"I thought you might like to wear this leather vest over your shirt, so you'll feel more comfortable in a leather club." Charles stood in the doorway, holding the vest.

Nathan did a double-take when Charles entered the room wearing tight black jeans, a black shirt under a leather vest, and leather kick-ass boots. He inched closer to Nathan when he stood.

"Thanks. I never wore a leather anything before."

"There's always a first time." Charles winked.

"You look hot in leather, and so different from your suit on the plane."

The way Charles changed his entire appearance by wearing leather excited Nathan. He wondered what he looked like in the shower. Even the wide black leather straps decorating both of his wrists excited Nathan. Charles Moore belonged in an erotic fiction novel as the main character. He was perfect, and he was giving him a chance. He wasn't worried about his lifestyle. Anything had to be better than hiding who he was.

"Thank you." Charles moved closer to him and helped him put the vest on. He wondered if he just wanted to be close to him and touch him. When he did, Nathan felt his pulse racing, which was crazy because the man only helped him with a vest, not stroked his excited cock.

"You look darling, and I mean that in a good way. I'm also surprised you're so open to exploring alternative lifestyles."

"That's because I didn't have a life before. I walked around hiding who I was."

"I used to be like that in high school, but unlike you, I caved in and married a woman. It didn't work out."

"Are you still married?"

"No. That's why I was in Chadds Ford. I had to formalize the divorce and my share of the property we once owned together."

"Did you have a house there?"

"On the hill. Moore Hill."

"Was your wife a teacher?"

"Yes."

"Mrs. Moore was my Trigonometry teacher." Nathan covered his mouth. He should have left that bit of information out of their conversation.

"It's a small world. Are you ready?"

"Yes, Sir."

"I see you've been reading the BDSM handbook."

"I found it on the bookshelf." Nathan pointed to the bookshelf beside the desk. "I hope you don't mind me reading your books."

"I'm glad you did. That's why there're books in here, especially for a special guest like you."

"Do you think I'm special?"

"Very."

They got into a red sports car, which Nathan had instantly fallen in love with. It seemed Charles had plenty of money and he wondered where he'd earned it. Did all his money come from teaching? He thought about Mrs. Moore. She was young and pretty, but Charles divorced her. He hoped she wasn't his competition, and that he didn't have to live up to her status. He didn't know how that would work at all.

Once they arrived at the club, a man parked the car, and they walked into the building. His nerves were working overtime when he saw all the men in leather. There was some music playing and a few men dancing together. Then he looked at the raised floor that had a bench. A young man was bent over, while this huge leather man paddled him. What shocked Nathan was the young man's ass was bare, his shorts were dropped to his ankles. The sound of the paddle pounding against his bare skin made Nathan's cock harden. What was happening here?

"That sub likes to be paddled. He could do it for the pleasure of the pain, or the Dom may be punishing him. What do you think of that?"

"I'm embarrassed to say. Do you think the Dom should punish him in public?"

"Depends. If they signed a contract and both agreed public punishment is okay, then he could. He may have broken a rule, or the sub might have asked for it because he likes it. Nothing happens to a sub without his agreement. And even then, the sub has a way out by using his safeword."

"That's fair. I wish I knew if the sub wanted that paddling."

"You could always ask him."

"He might tell me it's none of my business."

"I think he'd answer your question."

James and Tyler walked up to them, both also dressed in leather.

"Hey, you guys made it," James said, eyeing Nathan.

"Can I introduce Nathan to some subs?" Tyler asked.

"Sure, you can. Thank you," Charles said. "Don't keep him away for too long."

"I won't."

Nathan felt comfortable around Tyler so he would be okay.

They walked up to a young man standing beside a wall. He wasn't with anyone.

"Hey, Mason, this is Nathan. He's staying at Charles's place for now."

"Are you replacing Hans, or are you both going to be his subs?" Mason asked.

"Neither. Hans left Charles, and I'm not his sub," Nathan said.

"Hans left? Why?"

"I don't know for sure. Charles said he went back to the Netherlands," Nathan said.

"Then if Charles is available, work on becoming his sub. He's one of the best Doms around here."

"I'm new, so Charles is introducing me to the lifestyle," Nathan said, feeling a little out of his league.

"That's a big deal. He must be interested in you to bring you here. I've never seen him bring anyone here unless they were his sub."

"I think he is too," Tyler added.

"I wouldn't mind if he made me his sub. I know little about it, but I'm willing to learn more."

"If you hang around with us, we'll teach you how to make Charles want you as his sub."

"Thanks." Nathan scanned the room for Charles, and he was talking to a short blond guy. He looked troubled, but he didn't know him well enough to read his emotions for sure. He didn't like that guy talking to Charles. He shouldn't feel this way since Charles didn't owe him anything. All the good feelings he'd had sitting beside him in the sports car disappeared. Now, he wondered if Charles would ignore him to play with the blond guy. Their conversation continued for an eternity.

"Hey, do any of you guys know who Charles is speaking to?"

Tyler and Mason both turned their heads to the bar area.

"What the hell?" Tyler said.

"Yes, we know him. That's Hans. I thought you said he returned to the Netherlands."

"That's what Charles had said," Tyler said.

"Should we go over there and say hi?" Mason asked.

"I'm not going to say hi," Nathan said. He walked away from them in the opposite direction from where Charles stood with Hans. He had to admit Hans was adorable. Now, he had to fight off this jealousy. He wasn't used to feeling like this over anyone or anything.

BDSM activities and scenes were going on everywhere he looked; some looked fun, but others had to be painful. He took the long hallway with lots of doors. Each room had a window to peer into, but some had closed drapes. Through one window, he saw one guy bent over a chair, his head covered with a leather hood. Another guy was tying him to the legs with a rope. It didn't look comfortable. He waited to see what the guy was going to do. Did he do that because he wanted to, or to please the Dom?

Tyler stood beside him. "Hey, are you upset?"

Nathan faced him and said, "I guess I'm worried Charles will ask me to leave, and I'm a little jealous of Hans."

"The thing about this scene is ex-Doms and subs always show up when you don't want them to. The reason is that we're a small group. I saw the way Charles was looking at you. Don't worry. He'll take care of you. As for Hans, they're discussing closure."

"What if he wants to take Hans home with him? I should leave, right?"

"Leave to go where? Look, give me your phone, and I'll add my number. If you find you're uncomfortable, call me, and I'll pick you up. I know James would be okay with it."

Nathan handed his phone to Tyler.

"Can I give you my number in case you want to get in touch with me?"

Tyler passed his phone to Nathan, who added his number.

"Thanks."

"Do you want to check out the subs' room? It's called the Closet."

"Yes. Anything to hide."

"Follow me. Doms don't go in there unless it's an emergency."

"Good."

CHAPTER EIGHT

Charles

As soon as Nathan left with Tyler, he scanned the area to see who was there. He noticed a young blond man, who looked like Hans from a distance. He must be imagining it, so he turned to see where Nathan had gone, but he wasn't in view from where he stood. James moved to a table with another Dom to discuss something personal.

"It didn't take you long to replace me, did it?" Hans said.

Charles was surprised by Hans's appearance. He wore tons of eye makeup, and his ears were pierced in several new places as were his eyebrows. His leather attire was skimpy. The boy was on the make, and it made Charles sick. There was no reason Hans couldn't move on without looking so depraved. He cheapened himself. The little liar aggravated him more than he wanted to admit. The time they'd spent together was special, but he didn't have that deep love Hans had wanted. He could have stopped all of this if he had pretended to care more about him on an emotional level. In a way, he had created the downfall of Hans. He didn't like what he saw in Hans's expression, the hurt, anger, and the desire for revenge. This was all Charles's fault. Why didn't he expect this? For one, he believed he was back home in the Netherlands.

The disrespectful tone in Hans's voice made Charles want to discipline, but he wasn't his sub anymore, so he had no business touching. As far as he was concerned, their relationship had ended, unable to be mended. He wished Hans had gone home like he had said. He didn't want to confront him, nor did he want Hans ranting over the way Charles had treated him. He needed to leave and find another club. "I thought you said you were returning to the Netherlands."

"I changed my mind. I needed to see how long it'd take you to find someone better than me."

"I don't know what you're referring to, but who I see isn't your business. You left me a note and broke our contract. Never address me disrespectfully. Just move on. I'm no longer your Dom because you made that happen." Charles knew he shouldn't blame Hans, but his anger was eating him alive.

"You stand there fucking lying to me when I saw you with that guy. And that guy doesn't belong here."

Charles was fuming. If he continued talking to Hans, he'd end up doing something he'd regret. He walked away, leaving Hans standing alone. He wanted to spend time with Nathan. Since Tyler had said he was going to introduce Nathan to the other subs in the Closet, he made his way there with the hope Hans didn't follow him.

"Do you want me to get someone for you, Sir," a young sub asked.

"Yes, his name is Nathan, and he's with Tyler."

The boy left the hallway and entered the Closet. Within minutes, Tyler and Nathan came out of the room.

"I need to talk to Nathan alone," Charles told them.

"Yes, Sir." Tyler left them alone and found James in a booth.

"I'm going to take you in a private room to discuss something sensitive, not for anyone's ears but yours and mine."

"I saw Hans talking to you."

"I figured you did. That's something I want to discuss with you, but that's not all."

"Yes, Sir. I'll leave your home as soon as we go home."

"Who said anything about you leaving? Don't get ahead of yourself."

"I don't want to come between you and Hans."

"Follow me, and we'll talk. Nothing bad is going to happen."

Nathan looked miserable, like he was walking to his death. How was he supposed to trust him when Hans had returned?

"This is a private room where a Dom and sub play. We'll discuss all the furniture, spanking implements, and bondage items in a while. Sit on the bench."

Nathan obeyed his request but wouldn't make eye contact. The young man's expression clearly indicated he'd thought Charles was better or had a higher social standing than he. What did Lucas do to Nathan's self-image? Breaking eye contact communicated he didn't want to continue the conversation and desired some distance, which could be rooted in the psychological need to protect himself from expected embarrassment, shame, or other negative feelings that could come from the interaction. Charles better talk to him before he lost him. Something was wrong.

Charles sat down beside him so they were at the same level for their conversation.

"First, I like you more than I care to admit. When I first saw you enter the plane late and you were going to sit by me, I felt something immediately, even when you said nothing. There was something about your wild energy that got to me."

"Are you going to butter me up then tell me to leave?" This time, Nathan's sad eyes found his.

"Absolutely not. I know it upset you when you saw Hans. I'm sure the guys told you who he was."

"I asked them who he was."

"Hans and I weren't working out for a while, then he left while I was in Chadds Ford. Listen carefully to what I'm going to say."

"I'm listening."

Charles put his hands on Nathan's thigh.

"Hans and I are over. There is no longer anything between us. I want you to stay with me and explore what we could maybe have together. I'd like to introduce you to my lifestyle, but whether you want that kind of relationship is up to you. What I'm trying to say is that being my sub isn't mandatory for us."

"I'd like to get to know you more and I'm interested in learning more." Nathan's expression changed, his eyes sparkled, and he smiled.

"How about we talk about what's in this room?"

"Yes, that would be great."

"Remember, we're talking about what's in this room, not doing anything."

"But you said if I wanted to try things out, we could."

"You are very excited about this." Charles pointed to the spanking bench. "Let's check this spanking bench out."

They moved to the spanking bench area.

"So, we saw that guy on one of these. His Dom was spanking him."

"That's why it's called a spanking bench."

"Do you want to spank me on here?"

"You're so cute. I want to spank you and take you to subspace, but I don't think you're ready for that yet."

"Do you always know what others need?"

"That question would get you a spanking."

"Why is that, Sir?"

"Your question displayed a great deal of disrespect and deserves a couple of swats."

"Do it then instead of just talking about it." Nathan egged him on.

"Are you trying to get me to spank you?" Charles asked, wondering why he suddenly wanted to be spanked. Did the atmosphere encourage his sudden interest? He didn't know what he was asking for. He couldn't be serious; could he? His inexperience made any hopes of a serious response impossible, but he was obviously determined to gain Charles's attention, and he had. There was something therapeutic about spanking a boy.

"Yes, Sir. I want you to tie me down on that bench and spank me like we saw that Dom spanking his sub."

"Are you sure that's what you want, or do you want to fit in?"

"Fit in with who? I want this for me. I want to feel you touch me."

"I see. Let's talk about the rest of the furniture first."

"Talk, Sir? I'm ready now."

"You're not in charge. That will be your first lesson. I'm in charge and I decide if I'll spank you or not. I don't know enough about you."

"So, when you come here to play, do you know every sub you play with? I mean, everything about them?"

"No, I don't, but if they're here and have been around, I know they have experience with the lifestyle. I don't know if you've had any experience before."

"You never asked me. The other Charles was a Dom, and we did many things."

"And you call virtual experience true experience?"

"I don't know. I've never had any other chance. Now I think the other Charles took one look at me at the airport and ran the other way."

Charles saw the hurt in his expression and wanted to help him, but this wasn't the way. He inched closer and took him in his arms.

"You need comfort right now. You were hurt emotionally and physically. I won't contribute to it. I want to make you mine, but now isn't the time."

Nathan leaned his head onto Charles's chest.

"Are you going to tell me about the furniture in here and the things on the wall?"

"Yes. That spanking bench is for spanking like its name. The reason we tie you down is so you don't move while a Dom is striking your little ass because a sensitive area of your body might get hurt. I don't think you'd want your balls whipped, though some do."

"No, I don't want that at all." Nathan closed his eyes as if he were in pain.

"Do you see that large wooden X?"

Nathan nodded and pointed to it.

"That's the Saint Andrew's Cross where a Dom cuffs you, either direction, but mostly with your ass out. All kinds of play can happen when you're at my mercy."

"What if I wanted you to get me down?"

"That's where the safeword comes in, but if you want me to pause or stop for a minute, say yellow. If I ask you if you are okay, you say green."

"The traffic light colors."

"Yes. However, you don't have to use red as your safeword. It could be another word."

"I like the traffic light colors. It's easy to remember."

"Yes, it is."

"What is that?" Nathan asked, pointing to the sjambok hanging on the wall.

"That's a sjambok. It's made of heavy leather from Africa. It's about sixty inches long. Few Doms use it. One blow is more than you'll ever want from that implement. Are you interested in it?"

"Can I hold it?"

Charles removed it from the hook and handed it to Nathan. He ran his hand along the length of it and whipped the floor once.

"I think this would be too much for me."

"The sjambok wouldn't be the first one to try. A good old-fashioned hand spanking over the knee is where you should begin. Implements come later, depending on your need for pain. But when my hand meets your bare ass, you'll know it."

CHAPTER NINE

Nathan

Nathan didn't understand why Charles took him to the club if he wasn't going to play with him. All he wanted to do was talk to him about things, which didn't help his erection. When he thought about it, that's what Internet Charles had done too. He spoke of all the sexual things he'd wanted to do to Nathan, but in reality, it was all talk. He didn't meet him at the airport as he had promised. Charles was there for him to take, but he chose to walk away, or was Airplane Charles the Internet Charles? He had to wonder since both had money, talked about sex, but didn't take the opportunity to use him for sex. Why was it so difficult to get a man to fuck him? Charles seemed to like him, but then nothing came of it. That wasn't entirely true since he was now staying at his home. The challenge for him was to figure a way to get Charles to have sex with him.

"Is something wrong?" Charles asked.

"I think you're messing with me. You take me here to show me your world, and when I want to be part of it, you push me away. All you do is talk."

"We don't know each other yet. I don't know what you expect since we only met. Patience goes a long way."

"Are you open to questions?"

"Anything you want to know, ask me."

"How long did you know Hans before you had sex?"

"I met Hans here. I'd seen him around, and he was part of the scene. So, I took him home, and he never left."

"So did you give him his own room, or did he sleep in your bed?"

"Where are you going with this question?"

"I want to know if you took me in because you felt sorry for me, but you have no interest in me."

"I took you in because I care about what happens to you. I'm interested in you, but I want to be sure about you. Things between Hans and me didn't work out, so I'm not repeating what we did with you. There's an element of sympathy for your current situation, but it goes deeper than that. Give me time to introduce you into my world."

"So how long will this take?"

"I don't know. But there are some things that could speed it up."

"What do I have to do to make you invite me to your bed?"

"Something is wrong here. Why are you pushing so hard to get into my bed?"

"I'm nineteen years old, and I'm ready for it. I'm so done with talking. You're the same as the other Charles. All talk and no action." Nathan walked away from Charles and faced the door. Neither Charles took him seriously. He was tired of it all. He'd made a mistake trusting Charles. And to think he'd never shown his face at the airport. It had to be how he looked. His uncle had told him he looked like his mother as if she were ugly.

"I have an idea. Why don't we go home and cuddle up in my bed and get to know each other?"

"Can I sleep in your bed?"

"I'll think about it."

"What about playing in here?"

"You're not ready for that yet. I'm not touching you until you heal, and I know more about you. Let's go."

Nathan followed Charles out of the club to the car. He wasn't sure what to do about Charles. Still, he believed this Charles was the same one he had chatted with online. But that Charles went into far more details about sex, and this one talked around it. His doubts rattled around in his mind, leaving him feeling unwanted. Why was he taking his time with him but didn't do the same with Hans? He was so cute and irresistible. Nathan was sure it had to be how he looked. He was just ugly, and no one wanted him once they saw him in person.

Once they were home, Charles said, "Wait for me in my bed."

"Should I take off my clothes, Sir?"

"I hadn't thought about that. Yes. Take them off and get under the covers."

"Yes, Sir."

It was a good sign Charles wanted him naked in bed. This action moved their relationship forward and closer to Nathan's goal. He was way overdue to have sex, and Charles was perfect.

Nathan took the stairs to the bedroom. The colors weren't what he had expected. The black-and-gray themed room started from the large black floor tiles with heavy white grout lines framing them in place. While the tiles were undeniably dark, they were the shiniest floor he had ever stepped on. The white accents in the room matched the grout lines nicely, while the gray curtains were an excellent choice for the privacy he needed. The four-poster bed was perfect for Charles to tie up his sub. He quickly removed his clothes and slipped into the bed. The sheets were white but cold, not conducive for a hard-on.

The door opened with Charles walking into the room naked. He stood at the doorway and smiled at him in bed.

"Wow!" Nathan said.

"Do you like what you see?"

"Yes, Sir."

Charles made his way to the bed, then slipped under the covers. He sat up like Nathan.

"I know you've said before, but I need you to tell me the truth. Have you ever slept with a man?"

"Why is that important?"

"It's very important to me. Tell me."

"Could you tell I don't have much experience?"

"You never answer a question with a question when I ask the question."

"I want you to fuck me. I need it."

"You still didn't answer the question."

"I've never had sex with anyone."

"Thank you. Your first time will not be while you're hurt. But I want to start preparing you. Will you trust me to prepare you?"

"Yes, Sir. How long will it take?"

"It depends on you. Get on all fours on top of the covers."

Nathan pushed the covers off, followed the directive by getting on all fours, and waited.

"I'm going to lube your hole and put in a butt plug. That will stretch you so when we do have sex, it won't hurt."

Charles knelt behind Nathan. He put some lube onto Nathan, who was immediately shocked by the coldness. Yet, he didn't move, as he wanted to be perfect for Charles.

"When I first put this in it's going to feel strange, but you'll adjust.

"Yes, Sir."

"Are you sure you want this plug inside of you?"

"I want you to prepare me for you, Sir."

"Is that a yes?"

"Yes, Sir."

When Charles tried to push the lubed plug inside, Nathan screamed.

"Did that hurt?"

"Yes, Sir. But just push it in. I can take it."

Nathan watched as Charles lubed his own fingers, then slowly pushed inside Nathan's hole. He felt the burn and enjoyed the fullness.

"Your fingers feel much better than the plug. I like your fingers inside me."

"I bet you do, but I need to put the plug in so you can stretch over a period of time."

"Okay, I'll deal with it."

Charles carefully penetrated him with the plug. It took him a while to notice Charles was pushing in and out like he was fucking him with it. He had been feeding on the pain/pleasure. He enjoyed it. It was making him feel drunk. He panted, trying to get as much air into his lungs as possible.

"How does it feel now?" Charles stopped moving the plug.

"It's making my cock want to come, Sir."

"I guess it would. Do you feel comfortable stroking yourself off in front of me?"

"I'm naked, Sir. It's more of a need, and nothing to do about comfort."

"Lie on your back and stroke yourself for me. I want to see you come."

"Thank you, Sir." Nathan dropped to the mattress and flipped over so he could rub off. So odd, he used to do this for Internet Charles. There were so many similarities between the two.

"What are you waiting for?"

"I need some lube."

Charles smiled and handed him the lube from the bedside table.

Nathan massaged the lube on his hand, then every part of his cock, slowly rubbing, starting at the tip, working his way down over the base. If only Charles would do this for him. He was right there watching.

His cock twitched, reminding him to continue what he was doing, so Nathan worked his throbbing member with a rhythm. Once he began massaging the lube, he wouldn't be able to stop himself from coming. He imagined Charles flipping him over and sticking his hard cock inside of him. The thought of his pounding him made him come sooner.

"Oh fuck," Nathan panted as he came into his hand, Charles watching him the entire time.

When he was done, Charles got a washcloth and wiped him clean.

"You were perfect."

He bent over Nathan and kissed him behind his ear. His hands traveled over the side of his face and through his hair. It was as if he couldn't keep his hands away from him. Nathan loved Charles's kisses and touch. He wanted more, but he had to be patient until he was ready. After the first entrance from the plug, he believed Charles. He had to be ready for him as he looked at the size of his erection. Should he ask if he could suck him? He feared rejection.

"Thank you for giving me the gift of you stroking yourself in front of me," he said softly. He took Nathan's hand and helped him sit up against the headboard.

"I want to do more for you, Sir." Nathan eyed Charles's erection.

"What do you want to do?"

"Can I suck you until you come into my mouth?"

"Have you ever done it before?"

"Does that matter? I'll try my best to make you happy."

"You already make me happy. Give it a go."

Nathan grabbed the sack in his hand, licked every inch of it, loving the taste, then pulled one side into his mouth, carefully sucking, and licking hard. Charles's grunts morphed to moans; he swayed his hips forward as Nathan's lips sealed around his balls. Nathan crammed the other side of Charles's sack inside his mouth, careful not to bite. Licking and sucking as hard as he could as his own cock twitched and enlarged again. Nathan had watched many videos showing how many men loved to have their balls sucked, as long as there was no biting.

When Charles pushed his head back away from his sack, Nathan slid his hand back and forth on the hard shaft. It grew harder under his touch, rising and stiffening. He kissed the head, licking it and jammed his tongue into his slit. He tongued him, going in deeper and nibbling his clear juice, draining and swallowing.

"That feels so good."

"Mmm. Tastes so good, Sir." Nathan wiped his fingertips across his lips and tongued his lips in a circular outline as he lifted his head and gazed into Charles's piercing eyes. *He's pleased with me.*

"You like doing this for me?" Charles asked, stroking Nathan's hair.

"Oh yeah, Sir."

Nathan shifted his lips on Charles's cockhead. He liked the feeling of this man's cock swelling in his mouth. He could tell from Charles's moans he enjoyed Nathan's sucking, his head moving up and down on his firm shaft. He jacked Charles's cock with his hand, trying to stuff as much in his mouth as possible. He bathed the head with his tongue, knowing he was doing a great job as Charles guided his head, held between his enormous hands. Charles's fingers pressed behind Nathan's neck, ramming his head closer and closer until Charles's cock hit the back of his throat. His lips journeyed back up to the thick cockhead, tasting the clear juices. The tight skin of Charles's cock felt like velvet against his lips when he slid them across the head, planting kisses on the crown, and on the side of his hard cock. Charles encouraged him by pushing his hips forward, letting him taste his entire length.

Nathan accepted the shaft deeper into his mouth until Charles's pulsing cock head touched the back of his throat again. He fought the urge to gag. Of course, he worked against gagging. Never-ending clear juices trickled from the heads of both their dripping cocks.

Nathan's lips closed tightly around the base of his shaft. As he deep throated him, he gently caressed Charles's balls in both hands and forced himself to look into Charles's blue eyes. Sweat beads dotted his forehead.

Nathan trembled when Charles dropped kisses all over his head and neck. When Charles's balls tightened, he held Nathan in place, holding his head firmly, his cock buried in his mouth as Charles pounded against the back of his throat repeatedly, until he blasted deep inside Nathan's mouth.

"You did great." Charles put his arms around him and kissed him.

CHAPTER TEN

Charles

Charles woke up to his phone ringing. He turned to look at Nathan, who was sound asleep. He picked up his phone and left the bedroom.

"Charles, we need you to come in to meet with the trustee members in an hour. It's an emergency meeting," Dalton Smith said. He was the head trustee member and one of the largest donors for the West Mount Academy where Charles worked.

"What does it concern?" Charles didn't like the tone Dalton had in his voice. They had a lousy history together, and it sounded like it was going to get worse.

"To be honest, it concerns you."

"What about me?" Charles snapped.

"It's a sensitive matter and not one for the phone. We'll see you in an hour." Dalton ended the call.

He didn't like Dalton ending their conversation so abruptly, but it was expected. The man had hated him from the day he was hired as a teacher and wanted him fired a long time ago. His son wanted the position, and he'd figured he would look for ways to oust him.

He showered, and dressed in a dark suit, white shirt, and tie. He wrote a note to Nathan.

Nathan,

My work called me in for an emergency meeting. I'll be back as soon as it's over. I enjoyed being with you last night. I want us to work. Please be patient.

Charles

He raced out of the house and into his car. Normally, it took thirty minutes to drive to the school, but today he drove faster. He parked and walked to the Community Center, where they held meetings with the Board of Trustees.

When he entered the room, all the members sat around the long oval table. He wasn't late, but with all of them assembled there before him, he wondered how long they had been meeting without him.

"Thank you, Charles, for attending this emergency meeting on short notice. We're here to investigate a situation involving you," Dalton said.

"And what exactly are you investigating me for?" Charles was losing his patience with Dalton.

"All the members have received online gay chat transcripts of you and a minor. We'll be looking into this further. Until then, you're on paid leave. Once the investigation is over, then we'll vote on a resolution."

"I never chatted to a minor in a gay chat room." Charles stood.

"We have hard evidence. I suggest you get a solicitor to represent you. You're no longer permitted on the school grounds, including your office. If you want anything personal from your office, write to me, and I'll see that you get it."

"So, some trumped up charges are enough for you to place me on leave. This never happened. Someone else must have used my name. Do you have my voice or internet address while I was supposedly in the chat room?"

"We can't discuss the details of the investigation. But we believe you were in a gay chat room with a minor. This would disqualify you as headmaster and teacher."

"You'll be hearing from my solicitor very soon." Charles walked out of the room and made his way to his car. He couldn't believe what he had just heard. Having Nathan at his home would be the worst thing he could do at this time if he intended to keep his job. How could he explain Nathan at his home? Whoever had him dropped off knew exactly what they were doing. It had to be someone at the school who wanted him out. His first guess was Dalton.

He drove to a small café and ordered coffee. Choosing a booth away from people, he sat and called James.

"I need your assistance. Can I come over?"

"What's going on?" James asked.

"I'm about to lose my job."

"Come on over. I'm at the house."

He took his coffee with him to James's. When he arrived, James met him on the porch before leading him into his office. As far as Charles knew, Tyler was at work, so they were alone.

"What happened?" James asked.

"They said I was in a gay chat room with a minor. They have proof. What fucking proof could they have when I've never been in a chat room, let alone with a minor?"

"This is a setup like I told you before. And now you have Nathan living with you."

"And I'm not making him leave because of trumped up charges."

"As I see it, Nathan has to go. He can stay with us until things clear up."

"Thank you for your offer, but I want him with me."

"It may come down to Nathan or your job. See your solicitor and take his advice. I'm still having someone investigate the limo driver and who hired him. We need to know who set you up with Nathan. It all fits too nicely. No one is that good."

"What are you saying?" Charles knew what he was onto, and he didn't like it. They rarely disagreed on important issues, but he could feel this would be a big break between them.

"It looks like Nathan may be a part of the setup. How could everything fit so perfectly without him?"

"You met him. Do you think he's capable of that?"

"Anyone can pretend to be one way to hide their dark side. Just be careful where you go with him and who sees you. However, he's not a minor." James paused. "Was he a minor six months ago in the US?"

"I don't know when his birthday is, or if it was six months ago."

"Have you seen his driver's license?"

"No. Should I?"

"What if he lied about his age?"

"I hope he didn't lie about anything. I trust him, but I should've looked at his license to see his age."

"Tell him what's going on so he knows. If he is part of it, he'll stop and leave."

"You're wrong about him. He's upset he was left at the airport."

"Think about what you're doing. I'm worried about your job."

"I contacted my solicitor about the details of the situation. He's going to find out what they have on me."

"That's good. Lay low during the investigation."

"I will. Thanks."

WHEN CHARLES ENTERED his home, Nathan wasn't anywhere downstairs. He checked the backyard, and he wasn't there either. He climbed up the stairs and looked into his bedroom. The note he had left on the bed was on the end table. So, he'd probably read it. Empty. No Nathan. Where the hell was, he? He knocked on the door of the guest room, but no answer. He wondered if he went out with one of the guys.

Feeling a little grungy from meeting with the scummy trustees, he took a shower. The hot water cascading over his shoulders felt great. Feeling much better, he stepped from the shower and toweled off, wrapping the soft fluffy cloth around his waist, and walking back into the bedroom. He changed into a new pair of jeans and a shirt. Maybe Nathan had gone for a walk.

There was something about Nathan's desire to have instant sex. He claimed he'd never had sex, which knowing where he came from made sense. He had never seen such intensity like he had with him. What if he were part of the takedown at work? He walked into the guest room to see if Nathan left any information about him in his suitcase or backpack. He looked for anything that had any personal information, but only clothes were in the suitcase. He had his iPad and books in his backpack.

"Why are you going through my things?" Nathan asked as he walked into the room.

Charles turned around and faced him. "I'm looking for information about your age."

"I told you I was nineteen on the plane. Did you forget?" Nathan frowned, and Charles couldn't tell if he was more disappointed or angry at him for looking through his personal things.

"No. I heard what you said then, but I need proof. My work has accused me of going into a gay chat room with a minor. They claim they have evidence."

Nathan took out his wallet and pulled out his license. He inched closer to Charles, then handed his license to him.

Nathan had turned nineteen on March twenty-seventh. "I see you had a birthday a couple of months ago. I didn't want to go through your things, but I needed to know. As of today, the trustees have put me on leave from work until the investigation is over."

"Do you want me to leave?"

CHAPTER ELEVEN

Nathan

Nathan was disappointed to find Charles looking through his possessions without asking him. Why was he so worried about his age? Was he the Internet Charles? He certainly was acting guilty. Charles didn't answer his question right away. His pained expression troubled Nathan. He certainly didn't want to cause Charles to lose his headmaster position.

"I'm going to talk to my solicitor today. I don't want you to leave, but circumstances might change what I want."

"I'll just leave and make your life easier. Can you drive me to a hotel?" Nathan collected some of his things and put them inside the suitcase.

"I don't want you to go. Let me talk to my solicitor first before you decide."

"I want to leave now. You thought I lied to you about my age. I've never lied to you about anything. I've been open and honest in all our conversations, but the same can't be said about you."

"You don't need to leave. Come with me to my solicitor. I want him to meet you."

"I need to leave and think about what's going on here," Nathan insisted.

"If you leave to think, will you let me set you up in a hotel?"

"Why would you do that?" Nathan asked, feeling angry.

"Because I want you in my life. This way, you can call me anytime, and maybe you'll want to come back when everything is worked out."

"You can set me up since I'm not sure what I want to do." Nathan didn't want to spend money because Uncle Lucas would see him accessing his account. He didn't want him to know where he was.

"I really wish you would come with me before you decide to leave."

"I need the time. Give me your card with your number so I can call you."

Charles handed him his card, then Nathan handed him his, so he had someone to call if he ran into trouble.

"Meet me downstairs when you're ready. I have to make a call to the hotel first."

As soon as Charles left the room, Nathan went inside the bathroom and removed the butt plug. He cleaned it and set it on the sink to mark his place. Nothing was working out the way he wanted it to. Both Charleses wanted him gone, away from them. With all this rejection, he might leave London. He picked up his suitcase and backpack, then went downstairs to meet Charles.

"I've set you up in a nice hotel in London. You can do some sightseeing. Anything you want at the hotel will be taken care of by me. How much cash do you have?"

"I have two hundred dollars."

"Any credit cards?"

"Yes, Jacob gave me his to use. I can't use mine. I don't want my uncle to know where I am."

"Then you need pounds. I'm going to give you some for things you need."

"You don't have to feel like I'm your problem. You happened to sit next to me on the plane. You owe me nothing. I'm sorry I caused you problems with your job."

"You didn't cause me problems. The person who set me up is the damn problem and the one who promised you everything. Are you ready?"

"Yes." Nathan didn't like how angry Charles sounded. It felt like it was directed at him. Charles liked him until he was a source of his problems. It wasn't his fault this happened.

"Can I call you to see how you're doing?"

"Yes." He figured if he was paying for his hotel, he'd have to give back something. At this point, he wasn't sure about Charles anymore.

Charles drove him to London. He couldn't even enjoy the River Thames or the bridge. Everything he viewed blurred from the current state of insurmountable problems. Neither of them spoke in the car, all this tension ruining the drive for both of them. Shadows crawled over the car around them, and the tightness in the air made it hard to breathe. Nathan's doubts about Charles multiplied with time instead of lessening. Last night, he thought he'd made headway with Charles, and now he'd turned into Internet Charles by setting him up in a hotel. His actions were too similar to what he had gone through when he landed at the airport. At least he wasn't on his way home, but still, he'd wanted both of the Charleses, and now he had neither of them. He'd go to his room alone and decide what he should do.

How could he make a life here without being a citizen? All of this was supposed to have been taken care of by Internet Charles. Nathan wanted to find him and ask him what he had done wrong to cause him to abandon him. All those promises meant nothing to him. He made Nathan look like a fool. He was a fool the first time, and again he was a fool for this Charles.

"I'm going to call you after I talk to my solicitor. Save two hours for me tonight. I'll take you out to dinner."

"Why would you want to do that? Someone might see you with me."

"I don't care. I need to straighten things out so we can be together. Remember, I want you with me."

"I need to think about what I want to do. Nothing is going the way I had planned."

"Will you go to dinner with me?"

"I guess so. What time?"

"I'll meet you in the lobby at seven."

"I'll be there."

"Just tell them your name, and everything will be taken care of."

"You're just like Internet Charles," Nathan mumbled as he walked away from Charles. He didn't say goodbye or thank you. He was tired of Charles's double-talk.

Nathan registered at the check-in desk, and from there, the bellboy took him to his room. Once the bellboy left, Nathan threw himself on the bed. Things couldn't get any worse than they were today. Internet Charles had abandoned him, and now Airplane Charles couldn't wait to get him out of his home, stashing him away but pretending their separation upset him. He still couldn't help thinking both of them were one and the same. Too many similarities between the two. He no longer trusted himself to separate his feelings between them. His feelings for Internet Charles transferred to Airplane Charles all too easily. That's how similar they were. His emotions were all over the place, and he needed time to center.

The image of Charles going through his personal items burned what little trust he'd had, the same way he'd felt at the airport waiting for the love of his life. He never showed his face to Nathan. He still couldn't believe the man he had fallen in love with abandoned him, only to be stuffed into a hotel, then dumped off at Charles's house.

He called Jacob.

"Hey, how is it going?" Jacob asked.

"This Charles just dumped me at a hotel. It seems that his work put him on leave for engaging with a minor in a gay chat room. He went through my things, looking for anything with my age on it. I told him I needed to think, then he set me up in a hotel like the other Charles. Do you think this Charles could be the same one that was in the chat room and paid for me to come here?"

"This is getting crazy. It makes no sense. If he was the same guy, why would he not say so?"

"Mind fucking. I read about men who like to do that to other men. I'm an easy target."

"I wish you'd come home. Between those two Charleses, you're going to get hurt. I feel your pain already."

"My feelings are all messed up. I want this Charles, but I have to know for sure he's not the other Charles. And a part of me wants the Internet Charles. He seemed more interested in me sexually. I can't have someone fucking with me like this. I'm hurting, really hurting."

"I know you are. Did you ask if he was the Charles chatting to you?"

"I told him he was just like Internet Charles."

"Damn. I don't like the sound of this. Your uncle filed a missing person report today. It was in the local papers. The police paid me a visit and asked if I knew where you were. I said no. They left."

"Why did he bother? He should be happy I'm not around."

"Alma was over here looking for you too. She was very upset. I wanted to tell her you were okay, but she might tell Lucas."

"I feel bad she's upset. I wish I could talk to her, but like you said, she might tell my uncle."

"You're the talk of the town. There are posters of you all over, plus you were on the local news channel."

"That's just great. I wanted to leave without any fuss."

"It will die down at some point. What are you going to do tonight?"

"I'm supposed to go to dinner with Charles. He's going to his lawyer now. He calls him his solicitor." Nathan laughed.

"Go to dinner and pump him for information. Ask him some things you talked about in the chat. See if he answers the same way."

"Good idea. I need to know. A part of me wants him to be him, and another part doesn't."

After talking to Jacob, he took a nap, then later a shower. He went downstairs and out of the hotel to find a store to buy a nice outfit for the evening. He thought everything would have been taken care of, and now he was stuck doing everything for himself. He saw a store and picked out dark slacks, a gray shirt, red suspenders, and a black tie. Charles was generous to give him money and set him up.

After he stopped for a coffee, he noticed the lit-up London Eye from where he was sitting. It looked more like a giant bicycle wheel suspended vertically over the River Thames. While it looked similar to a Ferris wheel, it was nothing like the ones he had ridden as a child. For one thing, it was enormous—standing tall with an extremely wide diameter and was opposite Big Ben. The ride included one complete rotation, taking about thirty minutes. The odd thing was it never stopped completely when the people had to vacate at the end of the ride, but it was going slow enough they could exit without getting hurt. To make the time pass by, he counted the thirty-two capsules.

He wanted to ride it right now, but at the same time, he wondered if Charles would take him on it. He had another hour before they were to meet in the lobby for dinner. What if he didn't show up? He nearly drove himself insane with thoughts of further abandonment.

CHAPTER TWELVE

Charles

Charles waited for Jonathan to meet him in the outside patio of their favorite restaurant. He felt like an insensitive pig for not talking Nathan into staying with him, but it was probably for the best in the long term. None of it felt right, though. At least he'd see Nathan for dinner, then he'd bring him home. Thoughts of Nathan becoming upset from their abrupt separation and also from being dumped by the man he had fallen in love with disturbed him greatly. Right now, his mind needed to be on his meeting with Jonathan, not Nathan's issues. Like Hans, they'd both made the decision to leave him. He sucked at relationships. Sometimes, he wondered why he even bothered with any of them. Enjoyable playing with a sub didn't equate to a good relationship, but he wanted to change all that with Nathan.

When he looked up from reading messages on his phone, Jonathan took a seat across from him.

"I knew something like this would happen," Jonathan said.

"I ordered us beers. They're on the way."

"Thank you. So, do you have any idea who is using your name?"

"I don't know. It looks like it could be someone from the academy, but I don't know."

"I found out what they have on you. As they said, they have records of someone using your name in a chat room and claim the computer ISP address is yours. It's all posts, no pictures of you, but snapshots of naked boys."

"Anyone can change their ISP address to mine if they know what they're doing."

"I got your laptop from your driver, so my men are checking it out. I'll send it back when they're done."

"There's not a damn thing on that laptop that's criminal." Charles raised his voice.

"I'm not the enemy. Apparently, they're going for engaging with a minor, not the gay part."

"They could go for both. It's a private institution," Charles said.

"I know you wanted this position, but why there?"

"I always wanted to attend that school as a foreign exchange student, and it meant a lot to me to work up to the position of headmaster," he lied, but that was the story he wanted known. No other. His past must be kept in the past and never surface.

"Is Hans still living with you?"

"No." Why was Jonathan interrogating him as if he were guilty?

"What happened?"

"He left, that's what happened. End of story."

"Are you seeing anyone now?"

"Yes. Nathan Neumann, who I met on the plane. He was supposed to meet whoever was using my name. He never showed up, but a limo driver took him to a hotel, then the next day, he dumped him at my doorstep. So, he never met or saw the person. I had him at my home, but he's at a hotel now."

"How old is he?"

"Nineteen. Not a minor in either country."

"Why is he staying at a hotel and not your home anymore?"

"He was upset when I told him what happened at the academy. He's confused. I want him to stay with me."

"Who lives with you is your business and won't affect the case. However, if they go for the gay aspect, it could, but you had Hans living with you, and they never did anything about it."

"I'm angry that someone is trying to take me down."

"And what do you know about Nathan?"

"He's from my hometown. He left to move in with Charles Moore in London."

"So, he never saw Charles in the chat? And yet, he flew to London?"

"That's what he said. The limo driver dropped him off at my home. I never told him where I lived when we sat beside each other on the plane."

"That is one hell of a story. Didn't he know you were Charles Moore when you sat beside him? I mean, you must have mentioned your name, right?"

"No, I didn't tell him my real name. I never do."

Jonathan leaned back in his chair and shook his head in disbelief. "And he miraculously sat beside you? Maybe he's part of it?"

"Part of what?" Charles didn't like where Jonathan was going with his questions, but that was his job. His stomach contracted with anger when anyone blamed Nathan. If they only knew him, they wouldn't suggest he was part of it.

"He could have been hired to take you down. This story doesn't make any sense at all."

"No. Dismiss any thoughts of Nathan having anything to do with this. He's an innocent bystander in this mess. Leave him out of the equation."

"Be careful around him. Don't take him to any BDSM clubs. I'm working on the technical aspect, and I have my investigator researching the chat room."

"Thanks." Charles laughed to himself. Too late, he already had taken him to the club.

After he left the restaurant, he went home, and changed for dinner. He wasn't the kind of man who would be told what to do. Jonathan and James both thought Nathan had something to do with it. There was no way he could be involved. The poor, innocent guy was hurting, but he had to admit he was in a rush to have sex with him. Was he really a virgin? Charles knew that closed-minded community, and not many young boys would consider coming out. He certainly never did, so he believed Nathan, and no one would change his mind.

As soon as he entered the lobby of the hotel, he spotted Nathan talking to an older man. Nathan's stylish red suspenders drew attention, and he was not sure he wanted his Nathan to garner that kind of interest from other men, or women either. As he neared them, the two ended their conversation abruptly, with the man leaving immediately when Charles entered their private space.

"Who were you talking to?" Charles demanded. He didn't know anyone in London. So, who the fuck was he?

"Oh, I don't know who he is. He wanted to know if I needed help with anything."

"So, you don't know him?" Charles was suspicious of Nathan's answer. They had clearly been in a conversation.

"I don't." There was a glint of playfulness in his eyes.

"You look stunning tonight, so I thought he was hitting on you." Charles admired his black dress slacks, gray shirt, and black tie. Under the lighting, his hair shone more, and his eyes were glassy. Was he deliriously happy to see Charles, or was he high on something? In the few hours away from Charles, Nathan had erased his poor boy persona just by changing clothes. That too was slightly odd in itself. As he studied Nathan more, his hair almost looked like it had been professionally highlighted with blond streaks.

"Thanks."

Nathan smiled as if he had no idea what Charles was hinting at with the man. Could he be that good at playing innocent, or was he truly that way?

"What did you do all day?"

"I went shopping and sightseeing. I love it here."

"You do?"

"There are bright lights, clubs, and all kinds of people. It's so different back home. I could make a life here."

"We can talk about that. Are you ready?"

"Sure."

"I know a fun place to go."

"Thank you for asking me out."

They walked to the sidewalk and made their way to an area near the London Eye, going down a narrow alley to a large red ship.

"Where are we going?"

"We're having dinner on the ship overlooking the River Thames."

"That sounds romantic. You don't seem like you do romantic."

"You're kind of funny. I hope you're not afraid of ships."

They boarded the red ship and sat at a small picnic table facing the London Eye.

"Did you order tickets during the day?" Nathan asked.

"I did. It's a good tour of London."

"So, did you find out who is using your name?"

"No. I'm sorry I made you upset enough to leave."

"I didn't want to be the cause of you losing your job."

"Since I'm not going to be working, why don't you come back, and we can start all over again? I felt sad to see your butt plug left behind." He wasn't going to take no for an answer. He'd win him back before their date ended. Unfortunately, Nathan was an easy target due to his need for approval and acceptance in a foreign country. After all, he was all alone, and he probably didn't want to go back to living with his uncle.

"I thought you were done with me. I just landed on your steps. There's no reason why you need to mess around with me."

"Let me decide that. You can enjoy your time here and if you like it, then you can stay."

"I don't know. I need to think about what I want."

"But last night, you wanted me. Did that change?"

The server interrupted their conversation and poured wine into their glasses. Once she left, Nathan said, "I still want you, but I thought you wanted me out of your home since you were having problems at work. I don't like to stay anywhere I'm not wanted. I swore if I ever got away from my uncle, I'd never stay with anyone who didn't want me around. I felt like that this morning." Nathan sipped his wine.

"I'm sorry my reactions and words made you upset. I didn't mean to make you feel unwanted. And as for going through your things, I was worried about your age." Charles took two long sips from his wine glass. He had to make Nathan see his wrong as a right to make this work. He admitted to himself that he did overstep Nathan's boundaries, regardless of the reason behind it.

"One thing that is important to me is having my privacy. I was able to have some at home because my bedroom was on the third floor. My uncle came up once at night to make sure I was where I was supposed to be. He never hung out with me there. I had the entire floor to myself."

"Are you an only child?"

"Yes. I don't even have cousins or stepsiblings. My uncle didn't have children. My aunt left him because he was abusive."

"Why didn't you go with her?"

"She left before my mother and father were murdered."

"Explain this to me. If I want you, why are you running away from me?"

"I'm having a problem with going from the man I thought wanted me to you. I don't understand how I can feel so strongly for you when I spent six months with the other Charles."

"You transferred your feelings from him to me."

The server interrupted their conversation again with their dinners and a bottle of wine. She had a knack of coming to their table in the middle of an important conversation. However, delivering their dinner was her job, so he couldn't fault her for that poor timing.

"There's the Tower of London," Nathan said.

"It's a nine-hundred-year-old castle and fortress. Finish talking to me and explain some more."

"My other problem is I take what he said he'd felt for me, to you. He desperately wanted me sexually and talked about sex nonstop. We only posted about sex, no other conversations. When I'm beside you, I feel like those hot conversations were between us, but they weren't. In fact, you're not that into me."

"That's not true. I'm into you more than you know. I didn't want to make mistakes with you. Instead, I wanted to get to know you first."

"Don't you know me?"

"Not as much as I would like. Come home and let me show you my world."

"Do you mean handcuffs and blindfolds?"

"Bondage isn't for everyone, but if you want to try it, then we can."

"Do I have a chance of becoming your sub?"

"Of course, you do. But before that happens, we have to do a few BDSM scenes to see if you like it or not."

"What's going to happen to me after six months?"

"Is your visa for six months?"

"Yes."

"I'll figure something out so you can stay if that's what you want."

"Do you still want me when I think you might be the other Charles?"

"I know you have doubts and disappointments, but I wouldn't have hired a limo driver to pick you up. I'd want to see you as soon as I could." *The boy still thinks I'm whoever was Internet Charles and using my fucking name. Will he ever believe me?*

"I'm having a great time tonight with you. I still have doubts, but I want them to go away."

"It takes time. How about we give it a week for you to decide if you want to stay with me. This way, if you don't like it, I can set you up in the hotel again if that's what..." Charles paused. "So, do you want to move out of the hotel and come home with me tonight?"

"I'll give it a week with you."

CHAPTER THIRTEEN

Nathan

The dinner date was much more than Nathan would have thought. The scenery on the way to Charles's home was breathtaking. He was glad Charles took the time to check him out of the hotel and get his things. If only this Charles would be like the other Charles, then he'd feel he was wanted. Even that thought was naïve and stupid since Internet Charles hadn't shown his face. After six months, he'd thought the man was more than ready for him. Was he a pawn in another game? Were they both using him? His doubts returned even though he'd enjoyed one of the best nights in his life.

"Go to the bedroom and put your butt plug in. I want you naked, kneeling at the foot of my bed. Keep your head down and hands on your knees."

"Yes, Sir." This was something he had waited for. Now, he was acting like the Internet Charles, giving orders, and Nathan loved it. He wanted a man to order him to do things. He had no idea what he was supposed to do without instructions.

Charles went in the direction of the kitchen as Nathan took the steps to the bedroom. He didn't know where to put his dilapidated suitcase. It was rather beat-up and cumbersome, but he loved it since his parents had purchased it for him on the last birthday he'd spent with them. They had promised him a trip to Europe as well as many others. Unfortunately, he had never traveled with Uncle Lucas. He ended up using it when he'd stayed at Jacob's house. He'd never get rid of it despite the worn-out appearance.

The suitcase and backpack were going where he wanted to be. He set them down in Charles's bedroom beside a padded chair, then he went to the bathroom, leaving the door open in case Charles turned up earlier than expected. He removed all his clothes and carried them to the bedroom. He opened Charles's closet and hung his new clothes on the empty side of the closet to claim it as his. With little hesitation, he threw his underwear and socks into the hamper with Charles's worn clothes. He planned to make himself at home. He'd read about attracting and keeping love in your life. The author had instructed you to act as if you had the potential partner already. *Do those things to bind your love and care.* He thought the author had nailed love but fell short with Internet Charles. The author also wrote that no one should put all their eggs in one basket. So, he figured he'd follow his directions, but not the part of putting all his eggs in one basket. On the drive from the hotel, he'd decided to try to forget Internet Charles. He wanted this Charles and no one else.

Once he was done, he returned to the bathroom. He used the lube on the counter as he bent over the sink and inserted the plug. He could get used to the full feeling inside his ass, and it didn't burn as much as the first time. The sound of Charles's heavy footsteps climbing up the stairs alerted him to move faster. Nathan raced to the foot of the bed, knelt with his hands on his knees, then lowered his head as instructed.

Charles stood over him and touched the top of his head. He walked around him, touching Nathan here and there without any pattern. He'd read about Doms inspecting their sub. With great luck, Nathan hoped his body passed his scrutiny.

"I like you like this. Since you're in such a rush to have sex, how about tomorrow night?"

"What's wrong with right now, Sir?" Nathan read Doms got turned on by hearing their sub call them Sir. Some demanded it. That's what he wanted Charles to do. Nathan had issues with Charles's constant need to put things off. The man didn't take advantage of the present enough.

Charles rubbed his cock through his slacks. Clearly, he was hard. That was a positive sign. *Now get it out.* He'd waited long enough. Why wasn't he into him as much as the other Charles?

"Are you sure?"

"I want you to tie me up." Again, Nathan looked for signs of Internet Charles. He had told him he wanted to be tied up. Internet Charles showed him many different types and color ropes.

"Okay, if you want all that, then you need to have some directions on how we play."

"Directions to fuck me?"

"Once you go beyond vanilla sex, then there are rules. Before we play, I want you to understand you must use your safeword if you want me to stop. Red is your safeword. I might ask you what color you are at different points during the sex. If you're good, you say green. If you need a break or you want to talk, say yellow, and of course, if you want me to stop, say red."

"I can do that, Sir." Nathan thought this Charles was overboard on rules and directions. That had to be the downside of his teaching experience.

The directions seemed unnecessary for fucking, but the other Charles had also discussed the traffic light colors with him. He never used them, nor did Internet Charles ask how he felt. Until now, he didn't think his feelings counted all that much.

"Facedown on the bed."

"What about the plug?"

"I'll take care of it. Get on the bed." The tone of his directive indicated any further questions wouldn't be welcomed right now.

Charles sauntered into his closet, stayed there for a while, then he came out with a leather bag full of items. Nathan couldn't see what he was carrying. Charles didn't say a word about his clothes hanging in his closet. *Not one damn word.* Nathan had no way of knowing what his thoughts were on it, but since he didn't reprimand him, it must have been okay. Time would deliver its true verdict. Nathan didn't know this Charles well enough to determine his reactions to anything. For all he knew, Charles was using him to get over Hans. After all, Hans left him, not the other way around.

"Facedown. No one gave you permission to look at me."

"Sorry, Sir." Nathan put his face into the pillow.

Charles handcuffed his hands to the headboard, then he did the same with his ankles to the footboard. Nathan's cock hardened when Charles locked his limbs to the bedposts. He had waited so long for this, but worried Charles might forget about the plug and fuck it up inside him. Charles made it clear he hadn't liked his question about the plug the first time he had brought it up, so no way was he going to remind him again. *Take it out, damn it.*

Charles ran a feather up and down Nathan's body, tickling him.

"Are you going to tickle me to death?" Nathan wasn't expecting to be tickled, but he didn't know what he was supposed to do with it. The way Charles used the feather on him sent goosebumps throughout his body.

"I'm going to feather torture you for looking at me without permission." He continued outlining his back, buttocks, and legs.

Nathan sucked in a breath and arched into the touch while Charles used the feather on him. Charles had him in a fit of girlish giggles every time the feather touched him. He didn't know why but his cock tightened further. *Fuck, he's going to make me come from tickling my balls. Not now. Stop giggling.*

"Laughing is okay."

"Thank you, Sir."

"Do you want me to spank you first?"

"Yes, Sir. I wish you would."

"I'm going to use my hand to warm you up."

Nathan nodded yes. He had no idea why he needed to be warmed up for fucking, but he trusted Charles knew what he was doing.

Charles climbed on the bed, knelt at Nathan's side. He smacked him hard with one whack covering both cheeks. *Fuck it hurts.* His hand turned into metal as he spanked his cheeks a total of five times, then he returned to standing beside the bed.

"What color are you?" Charles asked.

"Green. Very green, Sir."

"Did you like the spanking?"

"Yes, Sir. But I wish it lasted longer." Again, Nathan worried about the butt plug. Charles must have seen it while spanking him, yet he didn't remove it. But he was careful not to spank near the plug. He imagined it moved further up inside him and having to have it surgically removed, but Charles was a Dom who knew what he was doing. He trusted he wouldn't damage him.

Charles stripped off his clothes in a mad rush, walked over to a drawer, and picked up a tube of lube and a condom. Once he fitted the condom on his cock, Charles generously lubed his own rock-hard erection. He returned to the side of the bed and removed the butt plug, setting it on the bed table.

"Wash your plug after and put it back in."

"Yes, Sir." Nathan relished Charles's sexual directives.

He rubbed lube around Nathan's opening and loaded his fingers with it as he slipped one finger inside Nathan's tight hole, causing him to jump from the cold feeling of the lube.

"You're still very tight. This is going to hurt badly, but the pain will subside. Are you going to be okay if it hurts?"

"Yes, Sir. But I haven't had more than your fingers or the plug in me before, let alone a cock as big as yours."

Charles skimmed his other hand along Nathan's cheek and down to his throat. He wanted to tell Charles how much his attention and touch meant, but words were impossible to form. He wasn't sure he was supposed to initiate a conversation. Nathan's breath caught in his throat. More than anything, Nathan needed this powerful man's bare skin next to his. He feared the pain from Charles entering all the way inside him. He expected the pain would be intense, but belonging to Charles was more important than avoiding the pain it would create.

The tip of Charles's hard cock head pushed inside about an inch.

"Ouch!" Nathan trembled from the pain and fear of what was to come when Charles filled him. He wanted everything from Charles, even not knowing what *everything* was. He needed Charles inside of him. "OW!" He burned inside badly, never ending pain. *Charles is way too big; he'll never fit inside of me.* He bit down on his lip. *Why doesn't he fit inside me? What the fuck is wrong with me?*

"Relax, Nathan. Take some deep breaths." Charles wrapped his arm around Nathan, lifting him up a bit and stroking his cock until it hardened. "It's going to be okay." He gently inched his cock a little deeper, and with that, Nathan let out a howling scream.

Charles pulled out damn fast. "Breathe, are you, okay?"

Nathan couldn't stop the tears sprinkling his cheeks. He desperately wanted to please Charles, not act like a stupid screaming child. He hated himself. *Why did it hurt so much? I'm too small for Charles.*

Charles stroked his hair.

"I want to meet your needs and be your sub like Hans," Nathan said.

"You'll meet my needs." He wiped Nathan's tears. "I got so excited that I rushed you. Do you want me to stop?"

"No, I want you to make me yours, but—" Nathan said.

"I've got an idea. I think the angle is bad for your first time." He unlocked the cuffed hands from the bedpost. He massaged his wrists, then he removed the handcuffs from his ankles. He massaged his feet until he could feel them again.

"Get on all fours." Charles helped Nathan into the position and forced his head to rest on the pillow.

Nathan bit down on the pillow hard, trying to muffle his screams of pleasure and pain as Charles carefully edged his big cock into his tight, lubed butt hole. Charles's thick cock stretched his quivering hole wider and entered further than he ever thought it could reach inside.

"That's it, love," Charles said. "Stick your cute little ass in the air. You have such a tight warm hole. I could fuck you for hours."

Nathan moaned louder as Charles's dirty talk excited him even more. "Mmm, yeah, your boy likes the sound of that."

The pain subsided when something glorious hit one spot inside his ass, exciting him, almost making him crazy with delight. Charles continued to stroke him, hammering that same spot. He panted and shuddered from the pleasure inside him. He was going to belong to Charles! He had wanted this, and now he was no longer a virgin. If he could shout it to the world, he would.

"Good boy. Now come on, open up that sweet hole, swallow my cock with your ass muscles. I'm going to go deeper inside you." Charles twisted Nathan's nipples with his other hand, bringing moans of pleasure from him. He shifted his hands, holding his balls while the other was pulling the foreskin back as far as possible. The pain and pleasure caused Nathan to moan with delight.

"Ahh—I'm coming," Charles shouted.

Charles flooded his cum in his condom, igniting Nathan to spill his cum in five quick spurts. Nathan made animal grunting sounds as his cum landed in Charles's hand.

"Ahh—you're so good, my beautiful boy," Charles said.

"Are you sure I was okay, Sir?"

Charles wrapped his arms around Nathan, rocking him. "You're my boy now, but not my sub."

"What's the difference?" Nathan closed his eyes in exhaustion and never heard the answer.

CHAPTER FOURTEEN

Charles

Charles woke up with Nathan beside him, still sleeping like a perfect angel. He hoped Nathan didn't have anything to do with the setup. Since he had done everything he could for now by hiring a solicitor, he wouldn't put any more energy into worrying about the possibility of losing his job to a lie. Of course, he realized private institutions ruled from within by affluent donors, making employee protections nonexistent. As he turned to get up, Nathan stirred under the covers.

"Good morning, Sir."

Charles turned around, bending over beside the beautiful young man in his bed. He wanted to breathe him, lick him, eat him, and drink him. His lips tasted sweet like honey. His face had the slightest bit of stubble, and it rubbed his skin, but he didn't care. Didn't care at all. He felt wonderful even with his world falling apart professionally. Charles moved his hands everywhere, and it didn't matter that his mouth was already on top of his—Charles wanted him closer, closer, and closer.

In the shadows, Nathan's face was so close to his that he could smell the sweet fragrance of the night, and then his tongue was in Charles's mouth. He wished to look at his face, expecting only the expression of delight. But he did not even catch a glimpse of his adorable face, so instantaneous and urgent was that tongue. Nathan wanted him again. Charles pulled back.

"Good morning."

"I want to do what we did last night again, Sir."

"I don't want to hurt you. So, maybe tonight if you're feeling less pain."

"Did you put the plug back in? I don't remember putting it in," Nathan asked.

"Yes, to stretch you so I slip right on in. I was upset I hurt you. I should have made you wait another day." Charles got out of bed and slipped on a pair of sweats.

"It's not your fault I came to your bed as a virgin."

"The good news is you're not one anymore. We'll make up for lost time."

"I like the sound of that."

"How about we have breakfast, then I'll take you to a BDSM store. Would you like that?"

"Yes. I've been to online stores, but never in person."

"I want to give you different experiences so you can choose what you want. Sex is new to you, and I want you to enjoy it as much as possible. Are you still sore?"

"A little."

"Turn over and I'll put some lotion on you. We'll take a shower after breakfast." Charles opened the bedside table drawer and pulled out some lotion.

Nathan flipped over and waited for Charles. He lifted the covers and gently rubbed some lotion on his hole. Nathan groaned.

"Put these bottoms on and meet me downstairs." He put a pair of sweats on the bed.

Charles went to the bathroom to wash his hands, while Nathan slowly got up and put on the sweat bottoms. He went down the stairs to the kitchen and made coffee for them. As much as he disliked tea, he missed watching Hans stirring sugar into his tea. He took the mug and put it in the cabinet. Nathan had probably seen it already. When he turned around, Nathan stood in the doorway watching him. He wondered how long he had been standing there.

"Sit down. I'm going to cook you breakfast," Charles said.

Nathan took a seat with a sassy smirk as if he had known he was upset about Hans's mug. Charles waited for him to say something, but he didn't. He smiled like he owned the world. He wondered if Nathan wasn't as innocent as he made out to be, then he replayed the image of him hurting when he entered him. He doubted he faked the pain or the intense expression he had. Even though he was innocent, there was a sense of pride in him. Certainly, he must have preferred others to think of him as accomplished in all things. Time would tell what Nathan actually was capable of doing in the world. He knew horses, but there were no horses nearby.

"Are you upset I'm here instead of Hans?" Nathan asked.

Charles stopped what he was doing, turned around, and said, "What made you ask that?"

"I don't know. People get used to a routine, and he was part of yours. Now I'm here instead of him. There's a break in your routine. I'm the one causing that."

"If I didn't want you here, I know how to ask you to leave. Hans is in my past, and you're in my present."

"And the future?"

"I don't know the future, but I hope you're still here with me. I like having you here." Charles set a mug of coffee in front of Nathan and kissed his cheek.

"Thank you. But I might not be as good as Hans in anything. He sure was cute."

"You're very hot! Don't sell yourself short. I love your dark hair and eyes contrasting against your light complexion. You're beautiful to me."

"Do you think so?"

"Of course, I do."

The doorbell rang. Charles left the kitchen to answer it. The first thing he did was to check the peephole. He wished he hadn't seen Hans standing there in black leather shorts and a vest without a shirt. His small chest was white and hairless. His straight blond hair was in perfect order with the addition of blue streaks running through it. What the hell was he doing here? He opened the door, and Hans smiled the way he always did when he wanted something from Charles. He had no damn reason for ringing his doorbell.

"What do you want?" Charles asked, glaring at him with contempt and suspicion.

"I forgot a few things, so I came here to get them, Sir."

"I'll mail them to you." Now, the little tart was calling him Sir because he surely wanted something.

"I know exactly where they are. It'll take me a minute, then I'll be out of here."

"Make it fast." Charles stepped out of the way.

Hans walked down the hallway to the kitchen with Charles behind him. He leaned on the doorway and watched Hans pull out his mug, then pivoted, facing Nathan, when he flung it on the floor on purpose. Nathan's presence startled him because it appeared he hadn't noticed him when he first entered the kitchen.

"Get out, Hans," Charles shouted.

"I see you have some little whore here to replace me."

"Shut up," Nathan said. "You don't know anything about me."

Hans moved towards Nathan, pausing to glare at him, then he took another step crowding him. Hans reached down and grabbed Nathan by the hair.

Nathan stood and slapped him with his open left hand full across the face. It rocked Hans and he took a step back then steadied himself, blinking his eyes and staring at Nathan. As Charles neared him, he noted Hans reeked of cheap alcohol. The boy was drunk.

"Leave!" Charles shouted again.

Before Charles could get between them, Hans hit Nathan under his ribs where the sternum ended. Nathan gasped as he doubled over and pitched forward onto the table. Within seconds, Hans pulled a knife from his pocket, aiming it at Nathan.

"You'll never have Charles. Never," Hans shouted with tears in his eyes.

Charles moved between them. He fought with Hans, grabbing his wrist with his left hand and removing the knife. Charles overpowered him, lifted him over his shoulders, and carried him to the front door. He put him down outside on the front porch. He noticed a limo waiting for Hans, so he didn't have to worry about Hans driving intoxicated.

"You're no longer welcome in my home. You could have hurt Nathan with that knife. You know nothing about him. Get the hell out of here, and don't ever come back."

"He's using you. He's a whore, and fucks everyone. He's going to ruin you and take all of your money. Just wait."

"If you come near my home or Nathan, I'll file charges against you. Now, get out of here before I hurt you." Charles stepped back inside the house, slammed the door behind him, and locked it.

When he turned around, Nathan stood there in the hallway, his face even paler than usual.

"I'm sorry Hans started shit with you. He won't be back here anymore."

"You got really upset with him." Nathan had fear in his eyes.

"Are you okay?" Charles didn't want to upset Nathan any more than he had.

"Yes, he knocked the wind out of me, but I'm fine."

Charles walked Nathan back to the kitchen. "I'm sorry this happened. Hans has never acted like this before. He had a fucking knife."

Nathan got the broom hanging on the side door to the porch, swept up the broken ceramic mug, and emptied it into the trashcan.

"You didn't need to do that."

"I wanted to, because you're so upset and angry."

"That little fucker lied to me. He said he left some things behind. Then he goes to the kitchen and trashes his mug in my kitchen and attacks you. I've had it with him."

"I don't like him, but I hated you getting angry. It made me afraid of you."

"Don't ever be afraid of me. Come here," Charles coaxed.

Nathan inched his way to him, and Charles took him in his arms.

"I'll never hurt you. Please don't be afraid of me. You need to trust me if we are going to have a relationship."

"I'll try, but you got so angry. I don't like Hans."

"You have no reason to like him. He hasn't shown his good side around you, and I doubt you need to see him again. If he goes to the club, we'll ignore him."

"I thought you were going to throw him out a window."

"I'm sorry you got upset over my actions with Hans, but he had to go. He knows he's not allowed to behave in that manner. He could have harmed you with his knife."

"Maybe he was upset I was here."

"Oh, I'm sure he was, but he left me, not the other way around."

"But if he thought you didn't like him, he had no other choice but to leave."

"Is there a reason you left home other than for the love of your life?"

"I left because my uncle would never accept me as I am. He never wanted to raise me, but he wanted my parents' home. He was my only family. So, he moved in with his housekeeper, Alma."

"I'm sorry you had to go through that with Lucas. I know he's homophobic. I guess Hans left because he was unhappy too."

CHAPTER FIFTEEN

Nathan

Later after they finished breakfast, they sat outside overlooking the pool.

"Do you like to swim?"

"Yes. We have a lake on our property, so I got to swim a lot during the summer."

"Are you feeling any better than before about us?"

"I'm worried you're going to throw me out when you don't want me anymore."

"Hans left me. I wouldn't have kicked him out like that even if I was done with him. The truth is, he was done with me."

"Don't you wonder why he acted the way he did today?" Nathan didn't understand why Charles didn't find a good reason for Hans to leave him. He acted like he didn't want Hans anymore.

"I don't understand his current behavior. He's not a violent person, and he never started a physical fight before. I don't know why he's behaving like this. He got what he wanted. He left. It was up to him. I didn't make that decision."

"He had a knife, and he wanted to stab me with it because I took you away from him. He was angry at me, not you so much. I think he would have stabbed me in the heart. He wanted me dead."

"I didn't know he had a knife on him. I wouldn't have allowed him in here had I known that. I have to say his behavior doesn't add up to his letter to me."

"I'm thinking someone lied to him about something you did. I think your enemy told him shit about you."

"I never thought of that, but who knows when someone is using my name to take me down. I guess it's possible."

"He seems to be in love with you. He's acting like a scorned lover." Nathan felt jealousy over Hans, especially after today. He was sure Hans loved Charles, but did Charles love him? He'd have to ask around to find out because if he still loved Hans, there was no chance or space for him.

"Scorned lover? Do you read a lot?"

"Yes, there's not much I can do when I'm home alone."

"Then you didn't go out much?"

"I got out. The only time I did was when I left my bedroom through the third-story window and had to use the nearby tree to get down. I'd go into the city with Jacob."

Nathan remembered Uncle Lucas caught him a few times and made his life miserable for months. That's what began his nightly checkups in his bedroom. He threatened to lock Nathan in the barn for a week if he ever caught him leaving from the window.

"What did you do in the city?"

It was obvious Charles wanted to know if he had more experience than he had let on.

"We went to gay clubs in Philadelphia, but just watched everyone," Nathan said.

"I had no idea you'd been to any clubs. Did you have fun?"

"We did, but then we had to go home and pretend to be straight. You know how boring Chadds Ford can be for single gay guys. There was nothing for us there."

"I felt like that when I was your age, but instead of taking risks like you did, I gave up and got married. It was one of the biggest mistakes I made. We weren't happy together at all. She basically lived her life separately from me as I did from her. Then just recently, we took the formal step of divorce. That's why I was in Chadds Ford."

"I can't imagine marrying a woman. How did you do that?"

"I'm bisexual. I like both sexes, but lately I prefer men over women. I lasted a long time in the marriage. But we have been apart for five years. She had a guy she met and wanted to marry. We divorced so she could."

"How long have you been living and working here in London?"

"I've been living here for five years. I worked as a teacher at the academy where I'm currently working, then they asked me if I wanted to be headmaster. I love the job and the academy, but now I might lose my job. I hope not."

"Then why don't you get rid of me? It can't help your case when I'm living here with you."

"I have a right to live with whom I want, but this is more about someone trying to impersonate and implicate me for some reason. You're not a minor so it doesn't have anything to do with you, except the part about you meeting a man using my name. Are the two connected? I don't know."

"I'd like to know where the man I chatted with for six months is. How could he say what he said to me and then disappear?"

"We both want to find that man. My solicitor is looking into it, so at some point, we'll find out. Be patient."

"I really don't have much patience at all on that subject. I left my home for him. He made so many promises to me. And what he actually did was expose me as the fool I am. That's what really gets me pissed off."

"I don't see you as a fool. I'm falling for you. There's something so special about you that makes me want to keep you forever."

"On the plane, you said I should get my life in order before I chase love. So, it's different now?"

"What's different is I don't think I really ever was in love with anyone. With you, it's so damn different. I'd take you even if you didn't want to be my sub. I don't know how to explain that to you, but being a Dom is what I'm all about. I'd do whatever you needed or wanted for us to work."

"Do you mean that or are you just saying it so I stay here?"

"I mean it. I want you that badly. I want you to be my sub when you desire it too. But I don't want to rush you into anything."

"That's the problem with us. We're different ages. I want things now, and you're okay to wait."

"Good observation. I won't do anything to hurt you. We'll see how much you like my lifestyle. I can move you along a little faster than planned, but I want you to want it for you, not for me."

"There're some things I didn't tell you when we met. I was afraid to tell you."

"Tell me."

"I've wanted to be a sub for a long time. Charles was my online Dom. He told me what to do, and I did it. Like moving here."

"An online Dom? That's interesting. So, you were his sub without sex?"

"Yes, he made me do things on camera, but I had to cover my face. I did whatever he told me to do."

"He used you for his kinks. He may like online relationships to get off. I'm sorry you couldn't have experienced a live relationship, but I'm hoping you will with me soon."

"I told you so you're aware of my experience in your world, but I was still a virgin."

"I was planning to go away to a BDSM camp. Would you like to go with me?"

"Would I be your sub?"

"You'll wear my collar, so no one touches you, but we have lots of things to work out first."

"I want to go. Were you going to go without me if I said no?"

"No, I would stay home with you if you didn't want to go."

"Do you trust me in your home when you have to travel?"

Charles remained quiet for a minute. He never answered a hypothetical question without thinking. Nathan liked that he didn't have ready-made answers for all of his questions. He appreciated the time he took to consider his answer.

"I'd have to say yes. You demonstrate honesty and trustworthiness. I listen to what you say, and I believe you, so I would feel confident that you wouldn't break my trust in you."

"Thank you, Sir. I appreciate you thinking about the answer first."

"I have a question for you now."

"Ask me."

"Do you feel comfortable with me in public?"

"Of course, I do. I'm proud to be seen with you, but I just wish we were a couple."

"We're moving in that direction. Let's take a shower together."

"I thought you would never ask."

"Have you ever taken a shower with a man?"

"I took a shower for Charles. He told me what to do, but he wasn't actually in the shower with me."

"Get upstairs, boy."

"Yes, Sir."

CHAPTER SIXTEEN

Charles

Charles entered the bathroom and relished the sight of Nathan's naked body.

"Do you want to play a game without sex?" Charles asked.

"Yes, Sir."

Charles undressed with Nathan eyeing him as he did. Then he pulled out a pair of handcuffs from the sink drawer and turned around watching Nathan's cock harden. His sparkling dark eyes widened in surprise.

"I want you to feel what it's like to depend on me. Are you okay with this? They are foam-padded, so they'll be soft on your skin."

"Yes, Sir." Nathan bowed his head.

He cuffed Nathan's hands behind his back, then turned on the water in the shower and waited for it to be a comfortable temperature. "Get in."

Nathan stepped into the shower with Charles behind him, guiding him so he wouldn't fall. He took Nathan in his arms and kissed him. "I love having you with me."

"I'm happy you took me in when I first rang your doorbell. If you hadn't let me in, then I would have been stranded. Now that I'm here, I feel safe and happy with you."

"And you do please me." Charles poured some gel onto his chest and sponged him all the way to his feet. When he went back up, he hovered over his balls, washing them, then moved to his beautiful cock. "You're half-hard again. That's good."

"I love when you touch me, Sir. I'm addicted to the way it feels."

The water rinsed all the suds from Nathan. Charles wrapped his arm around him, held their cocks together, and rubbed in a slow rhythmic tempo. Nathan's balls tightened up, and his cock stiffened.

"Don't come until I tell you."

Nathan grinned, the sexy kind. "No, Sir." Nathan's head fell back against the tiles, and by his expression, he was lost in all the sensations fluttering through him.

Charles stopped stroking and tightened his grip on the base of Nathan's cock to prevent him from coming.

"Better slow down, my love," Charles whispered in his ear.

"Damn it!" Nathan glared at Charles.

"You don't want to know what will happen if you don't." Charles laughed and fisted both cocks again. Nathan rested back against the tiles again, water raining over him. Then he looked up at Charles, who shook his head no.

"When, Sir?"

"Not yet." Within minutes, Charles's cock twitched, and he came. "Come now."

Not needing any more contact, Nathan blew his cum all over Charles's hand, jerking and twitching from the force of his orgasm.

Charles let the water rinse their cocks, and he squeezed some shampoo onto Nathan's beautiful dark brown hair with blond highlights. Nathan closed his eyes, avoiding the shampoo. Charles was careful as he massaged Nathan's scalp vigorously. When he was done, he held the hand shower, rinsed Nathan's hair, and brushed the tangles out with the brush on the shower shelf.

"Ouch! You don't need to brush so hard, Sir," Nathan said.

Charles swatted Nathan's ass with the back of the brush and left a bright red mark.

"Stop complaining. Oh, shit." Charles threw the brush outside of the stall.

He felt bad, really bad. He'd broken Nathan's trust in him. The boy wasn't his sub, but he was talking and treating him like he was. Sending Nathan mixed messages about their relationship was wrong on all levels. How could he have hurt Nathan and confused him? That was the last thing he wanted to do. Was he losing it with Nathan because of what he really wanted from the boy?

"I'm sorry, Nathan. I didn't mean to go all Dom on you when I'm not your Dom."

"Let's call what you did as practice for me, Sir."

"We don't practice. Either you're my sub or you're not. It's my responsibility to know the difference."

"Can I wash you now, Sir?"

"Wash me all over, pretty boy." Charles removed the cuffs and set them on the sink.

In the beginning, Nathan was hesitant when he washed Charles. He didn't press hard as he scrubbed his back, then he moved down to his ass and cleaned it inside and out. He was so careful when he washed his balls. He managed to wash his hair and rinsed it. They exited the shower and got dressed.

IN THE CAR, NATHAN sat a little closer to him and smiled more during the trip to the BDSM store. He was clearly excited about this trip. Charles wanted to buy him everything in the store. He knew he shouldn't spoil him, but Nathan needed someone to care for him. With all the disappointments he'd faced after his trip, he had to experience being free, safe, and loved. Loving him this soon was so unlike Charles. At this point, he couldn't imagine living without him. Nathan had taken over Charles's feelings without permission. Yet, Charles's love poured out around the beautiful boy without understanding anything about him. It just happened. Neither of them had done anything to facilitate the love Charles had felt upon meeting him on the airplane.

"I'm really excited," Nathan said.

"That's what I love to hear."

From the outside, it looked like a regular store. As soon as Charles parked the car in the lot, they walked into the building. They were greeted with sensual music mimicking the sexual act. "Are you sure you're okay being inside here?" Charles asked Nathan.

"Yes, I want to be here with you. Don't you?"

Charles winked. "Let's find some toys."

A slow, naughty smile spread over Nathan's handsome face. Charles's body ached for Nathan's. The store, the talk of BDSM, and Nathan; it all reminded Charles how much he had enjoyed being a Dom. However, he had no idea if Nathan would enjoy the role of a sub. He didn't know enough about him, even with his admission about his Internet Charles taking an online Dom role with him. Yet, he was a virgin before he arrived in London. Something was amiss, but he couldn't put his finger on it.

The first area carried all the foreplay goodies, lubes with different flavors, and some edible or warming varieties. There were two couples around the spanking implements.

"I don't have anything new to spank you with," Charles said. He walked over to the spanking implements and picked up a flogger. "What do you think of this for when we play?"

"I don't know how it feels, Sir." Nathan rolled his eyes then grinned.

Charles slammed the flogger across Nathan's ass. His face turned red, and then he laughed.

"Well, did it feel good?" Charles asked.

"I felt it, so it must be good."

"Good because I'm going to buy it. Maybe tonight I'll try it out."

"I think you already tried it out."

"Maybe you can get into subspace with it," a young man said.

"Subspace?" Nathan asked.

"We'll talk about that later," Charles said.

The taller man dressed in leather picked up a flogger and swung it at the ass of the young man who had spoken to Nathan. "Mind your own business, boy."

"Yes, Sir."

"Let's look at those paddles," Charles said.

"Yes, Sir."

"Are you sure?"

"I trust you," Nathan said.

"Trust is the most important element in a BDSM relationship."

"What else are you going to get?" Nathan asked.

"Tell me what you want," Charles responded.

"I want you to get rope so you can tie me up." Nathan's cheeks reddened.

Charles picked up handcuffs, rope, and a spreader. They stood in front of the wall of paddles. He picked out one covered with red leather.

"Do you like this one?"

"I don't know. Could you try it out on me, Sir?"

Charles laughed. "You're making this trip fun." He inched closer to him. "Bend over the table."

Nathan did as he was told, and it made Charles so happy. He couldn't believe how much fun Nathan was. He liked when Charles spanked him in public. Good to know.

"Why does that man have a leash on his sub?"

"He wants his sub to be submissive to him in public. Why, do you want me to put a leash on you?"

"I'm not going anywhere without you, but I wouldn't be against it at the club," Nathan said.

Charles went to the other side of the store and picked out butt plugs including vibrating ones, warming lotion, a cock cage, and nipple clamps. He had all these play items in his playroom, but he wanted Nathan to have his own, not hand-me-downs from Hans. He planned on donating those to the club. He picked out some chaps and vests for Nathan. He took him to the boot area.

"Do you want a pair of these black boots?"

Nathan picked up the boot and rubbed his fingers along the top.

"Yes, Sir. Thank you."

"I want to make you happy."

"Are you going to paddle me?" Nathan asked.

"We'll talk about that tonight."

CHAPTER SEVENTEEN

Nathan

Nathan waited on the porch while Charles made a phone call in his office. He had never been in that room because he locked the door when he wasn't in there. What did he have in that office that no one was to see? He wanted to know, and he also wondered why Charles hadn't taken him to his playroom. Surely he had taken Hans in there for games, but Nathan obviously didn't qualify to go in there. What did he have in there that he couldn't see? Charles had some secrets, but the biggest one had to be how he came by so much money. He'd worked as a teacher at the academy for at least five years, so he couldn't have earned it by teaching. The headmaster position might pay him well, but this house was expensive, and his sports car too. He didn't look like he needed to work if he lost his position. He never discussed money at all and why would he unless he had something to hide?

Charles carried two drinks outside and handed one to him. He sat beside him in a similar chaise lounge.

"Thanks." Nathan was surprised Charles had made fresh lemonade, something he loved in the summer. The other Charles had known about that, but this one didn't. Yet, here he was, making him his favorite summer drink. It could be a coincidence, or this Charles and the other one could be one and the same. Both were Doms and both were control freaks. What would he do if this Charles was Internet Charles? At this point, he was in love with both of them, so either would do. However, if they were one person, then he'd be okay with it, or maybe he wouldn't. He was so turned on with this Charles.

"I wondered where you were." Charles had that look in his eyes. He was pleased with something. Nathan only hoped it had to do with him and not Hans.

"I like it out here. It's quiet and peaceful, away from the city noise."

"I thought you liked London."

"I do, but I only want to go there now and then."

"How would you like it if we go riding tonight with James and Tyler?"

"Horses?"

"Yes. I know a ranch not too far. I thought you'd like that."

"I would. Thanks for asking me."

"We're going to have dinner after we ride, so put on some jeans."

"I hope you don't mind, but I moved into your closet and hopefully your bed." Nathan feared Charles's response. What if he became as angry as he was with Hans? He had to know what Charles's anger points were. He didn't want Charles throwing him out the front door like he had with Hans.

"I noticed that last night." Charles nodded with approval. His sexy grin told Nathan everything he needed to know. He wasn't angry about it.

"So, are you okay with that, Sir?"

"I loved it when I saw your new outfit hanging in my closet. It looked good in there and made me smile. I want you in my bed. I'm glad you read my strong feelings for you."

"I'm relieved you aren't pissed at me for not asking your permission. I realized later, I should have asked first."

"In most cases, I prefer you ask my permission before you take matters into your own hands. That is a must in a BDSM relationship, but we don't have one yet. So, I'm okay with it."

"If I were your sub, would you be angry at me?"

"Yes."

"As angry as you were with Hans?"

"No. Hans isn't your problem. Please remember that."

"He's my problem when he tried to stab me. I was probably sitting in his chair, in your kitchen, where he thought he should be instead of me."

"He won't be a problem anymore because I'll do what I have to so he'll never attack you again."

"Thank you for making my safety your priority, Sir."

"Are you upset about something?"

"It's my circular thoughts that hound me about you and Internet Charles."

"I see. What can I do to make those thoughts stop?"

"You could make me your sub."

"We haven't gone over anything yet, and we need to do some scenes together."

"Another thing that bothers me is you never showed me your playroom. I know Hans must have played in there with you, but I feel like I'm not good enough."

"We can fix that right now. I'm sorry I never thought about it since we haven't had a detailed conversation and to be honest, I didn't want to frighten you."

"I don't scare easily."

"Good. Let's go upstairs and I'll show it to you."

Nathan popped out of his lounge chair with great excitement. The man was finally taking him seriously. He'd figured he'd have to push his way into a BDSM relationship with Charles before Hans showed up again and convinced Charles to take him back. Nathan's fear of Hans replacing him was real and alive after he bore the brunt of Hans's erratic behavior. Of course, if Hans were successful, he'd be out on the street or worse yet, on his way home.

"I'm pleased to see you're excited about seeing the playroom. This really pleases me."

"And as your sub, pleasing you would be paramount to the relationship, right?"

"That's exactly right, but only after we both agreed to a contract on how we would conduct our relationship."

"When can we talk about that then?"

"Not so fast. Relax. We have plenty of time."

"I don't, Sir. My six months will be up quickly."

"Let's not worry now. I'll take care of your residency when the time comes. I know some people who can help us with that. How about a piggyback ride upstairs?"

"I'd love to."

Charles stooped so Nathan could wrap himself around his back. No one had ever let him do this before. Charles stood and climbed the stairs. He walked to the door at the end of the hallway, unlocked it, and set Nathan inside.

"Usually, you'd be naked when you come in here to play. But you're getting a personal tour. What do you think?"

"It's so big, I mean it's huge. All this furniture and spanking things on the wall like at the club. I wish you'd spank me on that bench." Nathan pointed to the spanking bench.

"All in good time. Walk around and touch whatever you want."

Nathan wanted to try everything out today. These were all the items Internet Charles had shown him in the chat room. He looked at the different paddles to see if any of them looked exactly like the ones Internet Charles had on his wall. He ran his hand over the leather and wooden one, but none looked exactly the same. He saw the St. Andrew's Cross, which seemed similar. Both were made from wood and painted black. The room had been a bit different to this one.

"What are you looking for?"

"Everything, Sir. I feel drunk from everything in here."

"Something else is going on. Tell me." Charles stopped him and made him face him.

"The other Charles showed me these types of paddles and a St. Andrew's Cross like yours. It makes me wonder what's going on."

"If he used my name, then he researched me. Most Doms have similar items. But do you see anything in here that is exactly like what he had shown you?"

"No. I don't. But..." Nathan stopped himself from saying, *but you could have changed things so you could make me think you're not him.*

"Nathan, it's going to take time to get over him. Remember he didn't come to the airport as he had agreed. He broke his agreement. A real Dom wouldn't do that to you. He conned you to get at me for some reason."

"But you sat beside me. That's kind of odd."

"I bought my ticket a long time ago. I had a sub living with me at the time. I'm not that Charles, but I know you're still working that out in your mind. This playroom hit some areas that brought him to your mind again."

"Do you have any enemies from your past?"

"I suppose I have hidden enemies. If I knew who they were, I'd confront them."

"Can I try that St. Andrew's Cross, Sir?"

"Stand in front of it."

Nathan raced over to the cross almost slipping on the wooden floor. He stood waiting for Charles to tie him up.

"I'm going to use metal handcuffs to bind you to the cross. If you want to get off, use your safeword, red."

"Yes, Sir. Will you use something on me?"

"Face it and spread your arms and feet wide, so I can cuff you. I don't like swinging at moving targets."

Nathan followed the directive. Charles fastened his wrists first, leaving him standing tiptoe on the wood floor. He clicked the leather cuffs to his ankles on both sides of the cross. Nathan tried to move and was unable to. His ass cheeks clenched at what was to come. He was more excited than anything else.

"Ten swats," Charles said.

"Thank you, Sir." Nathan felt trapped, out of control, just the way he had when Uncle Lucas locked him in one of the barns for punishment. On one level, he hated Uncle Lucas when he disciplined him. He knew there were times he had deserved it, but he couldn't control the festering hatred. He wanted Charles to give him pain. It was more sexual than punishment with him.

"Remember, if you want me to stop, use your safeword, red." Charles reminded him again softly, almost a whisper.

"Yes, Sir." He couldn't think clearly. He needed to calm down, take some deep breaths like Charles had told him during their first sexual encounter. He had never been handcuffed to a big X with his feet dangling. Something about this cross excited him. Nathan was unable to move in any direction with hands or feet. Sweat poured down his face. He had told the other Charles he wanted to play on one of them one so many times, and now his dream manifested into a reality.

"Your reactions belong to you."

"Why didn't you strip me, Sir?"

"You are not my sub."

Charles stood to the side and rubbed his back and spoke in a soft tone. "Nathan, I'm going to use a flogger."

"Thank you, Sir." He wanted to feel the flogger, but he wished he was naked.

"Stop trying to wiggle your way out of the handcuffs. You can't. Don't waste your energy."

Startling Nathan to reality, the flogger met his ass. He jerked from the unexpected blow landing hard. The thunderous thud pierced through his thoughts. The flogger packed a bite as it pelted against his jeans, the leather burning. Nathan bit his lip. The pain exploded right through his jeans.

It stung like a motherfucker, but his cock loved it. He felt it hardening.

Charles thumped the flogger against Nathan's ass without breaks between blows. Nathan twisted his head to see the flogger moving over his entire backside. Each blow tore into him and stung. With each swat, the flogger covered his entire buttocks at once. He lost count of how many times it fell on his bottom.

With what seemed like non-stop flogging, Nathan felt the heat and the sting. It moved deep inside his muscles and nerve endings. His ass cheeks jiggled from the impact of the blows. Wiggling around to escape Charles's big crippling flogger was useless, since he was handcuffed to the cross.

"Please fuck me, Sir."

"You need to heal first." He unlocked the cuffs and helped him from the cross.

"Yes, Sir."

"Follow me."

He walked with Charles to the little refrigerator where he pulled out a bottle of water and handed it to Nathan.

"You did very well. I think we're going to be doing a scene soon."

CHAPTER EIGHTEEN

Charles

They sat in the front room drinking protein shakes. Nathan was far more ready to be a sub than he had thought. After all, Nathan hadn't been upfront about his online BDSM experience, even though it was only a virtual relationship. He really played the innocent virgin like a pro. Was he part of his downfall? It was rare that anyone played him for a fool. *Not my Nathan. Please, not my Nathan.* He wouldn't believe it even if it were true.

Charles set his drink on the coffee table when he heard vehicles driving up in front of his home. He peered out the window and saw the police parking their vehicles. He felt sick to his stomach. Shortly, they pounded on his front door.

"The police are here. Go upstairs to one of the bathrooms. Lock yourself in there and don't open it."

Nathan frowned, disturbed by Charles's directive, leaving him frozen in his chair and unable to leave.

"Now!" Charles ordered.

When Nathan finally moved and hesitantly climbed the stairs, Charles answered the door, filled with anger.

"We're here with a warrant to go through your home," one of the officers said as he handed Charles the warrant.

He stepped back and allowed a group of them inside. He had heard of these police invasions, which normally left homes in complete disarray. He called his solicitor, Jonathan.

"What's up?" Jonathan asked.

"The police are here with a warrant searching my home."

"I'll be right over there to make sure they keep it legal." He ended the call.

Charles watched them opening and emptying drawers as he walked through his house. *What the hell were they looking for?* Then he thought about Nathan locked in a bathroom, or he hoped he was. He heard them pounding on a door upstairs and raced up there to make sure Nathan was okay. He had told him not to answer the door. Maybe that wasn't the best thing to do.

By the time Charles made it upstairs, they had broken down the door to get in. Nathan was squatting in the corner of the shower stall.

"Who are you?" one copper asked.

"Nathan Neumann." Nathan's voice trembled as he stood.

"Why were you hiding in there with your clothes on?"

"I was going to take a shower, sir." Nathan leaned against the tile.

"Why are you in Charles's home?"

"I'm visiting. That's all."

"He's my guest," Charles said.

"Show me your visa." The copper shot Charles a nasty look.

They left the bathroom and waited in the hallway for Nathan to fetch his visa.

Nathan returned to the hallway and handed it to the copper. He read it, then returned it to Nathan.

"Nathan, sit outside by the pool. You don't need to be in here," Charles said.

Without saying a word or making eye contact with Charles, he left them and raced down the stairs.

"How long is this going to take?" Charles asked.

"As long as we need it to."

"What are you looking for?"

"This is in reference to engaging in a gay chat with a minor."

"That never happened."

"That's what they all say."

Charles was losing his patience and wanted to punch the officer in the face. He wondered if someone from his past had initiated this bullshit against him. That was the point of moving to the UK. There was one friend who would know if something was going down involving him. That guy would have already notified him so he could make better choices in this situation.

Jonathan found him upstairs. "I talked to the lead officer and they're looking for pornography."

They broke into his playroom. Two policemen went in there with cameras and moved everything out of order. He heard them snapping pictures. His job was gone.

"They're in my playroom taking fucking pictures."

"This all happened so fast. They believe you were taking pictures of naked boys."

"No. There are no naked pictures of boys anywhere in my home or on my older computers."

They carried out two computers and one laptop.

"None were on your other laptop that I received from your driver."

"I don't want to stay here right now."

"Why don't you and Nathan leave, and I'll close up. I'll call your cleaning lady. She can put things back together."

"Thanks." Charles went to his room and packed a few clothes for him and Nathan.

He carried the suitcase to the backyard where Nathan was. He was playing with his phone.

"Hey, we're going to get out of here for a couple of days."

"Okay."

"I packed your things."

"Thanks. Are you upset with them going through your things?"

"Yes. That's why we need to get out of here."

Nathan followed Charles to his car and got in the passenger side.

"I'm sorry you had to be questioned."

"It's not your fault. It's whoever impersonated you in the chat room."

"I don't know who would do this to you or me. Your life and mine weren't connected. So, whoever hurt you may not want to hurt me, but they are. It just doesn't make sense."

"I wondered if my uncle had anything to do with it."

"Your uncle has nothing to do with me. We're not enemies."

"Where are we going?"

"To my cottage by the sea."

"You have a cottage too?"

"Yes. I have properties in different countries."

"Why do you have so much money?"

"I inherited it." Charles didn't like anyone asking him about where he had gotten his money. Of course, Nathan was curious, and he was astute enough to see his possessions didn't reflect his income. There was a lot Nathan didn't know about his past or how he came by so much cash to live comfortably in another country.

THEY DROVE FOR TWO hours then finally they reached the stone cottage.

"This is my English cottage. I know you'll like it here."

"I do. Why don't you live here?"

"It's too far from the academy. However, if things go against me, I might move here."

"If you don't have a job, can you stay here?"

"I won't be out of a job for long if that's the case." Soon, he would have to tell Nathan everything or lie to him. He wasn't sure if he could trust him with his past.

"Would you ever go back to the US?"

"I don't know. Do you want to go back?"

"No. But I don't think they'll let me stay here."

"Let's go inside. We'll talk about our relationship."

"Are you going to dump me?"

"I said talk about our relationship. How do you get dumped out of that?"

"I expect it, that's why."

Charles took him inside and put the suitcase in the bedroom. It was just as he had left it. The cleaning lady maintained it once a week when he was away. She did a great job, and he was grateful to her.

"Wow, it's so comfy in here."

"Let's go in the kitchen and have something to drink while we discuss our relationship."

Nathan followed him to the kitchen and sat down on a stool. Charles made them some lemonade then sat across from Nathan. Luckily, there had been some left-over lemonade powder in the pantry.

"Don't look so upset. The worst part is over with the cops. You said more than once you want to be my sub. Do you still feel that way?"

"Yes. I want you to be my Dom. I'll do whatever you say. I won't be a problem."

"You're not a problem. I love spending time with you. If you truly want to be my sub, we have to discuss my rules and consequences. You need to know what I expect if you choose to be my sub."

"I'm listening, Sir."

Calling him Sir put a smile on Charles's face. How he loved the sound of the word Sir coming from Nathan.

"I have five rules." Charles got up and pulled a notebook out of the drawer with a pen. He wrote the five rules, then handed Nathan the notebook. "Read them to me."

"Rule one: Obey me.

Rule two: Be respectful.

Rule three: No lying or cheating.

Rule four: Accept your punishment.

Rule five: Master Charles has the final say."

"Do you have any questions about my rules?" Charles asked.

"Any punishment?"

"Your punishment will be based on your limits. I'll ask you some questions to find out what your limits are. I'll never use a punishment that isn't within your limits. None will be your hard limits."

"That doesn't really say what you're going to do with me if I break a rule, Sir."

Charles took the notebook and wrote down a list of limits and spanking implements.

"Check off the ones you are okay with. Then circle the ones you never want to do or never want me to use on you. If you don't know what it is, ask me." He handed Nathan the notebook.

"Yes, Sir." Nathan read the items and made marks on the paper, then returned it to Charles.

"Very good. I'm glad you didn't circle everything, but if you did, then that's what we would agree to. So, you never want me to use a whip?"

"I don't think I'm cut out for that, Sir."

"But you're okay with paddles, floggers, belts, and my hand?"

"Yes, Sir. Can I use my safeword if I can't take it?"

"Yes, of course. Anytime, but if it's for punishment, then you'll have an alternative punishment."

"Can you explain what you expect from me as a sub?"

"I expect you to serve, obey, and please me. All of which you do so far. If you break the rules, I'll punish you."

"Thank you for explaining it to me."

"You'll wear my collar in the house and out to clubs, but not anywhere else."

"Do you have a collar for me?"

"I packed it. It's not the permanent one. I have to make it, and tomorrow we'll go out to get some leather. I want you to have one I made not bought." He watched Nathan break into a full smile. He wore all his emotions on his face.

CHAPTER NINETEEN

Nathan

Charles instructed Nathan to remove all his clothes and kneel in the middle of the room while he was waiting. It seemed quite impossible he was getting what he'd wanted. Originally, he thought he'd be the other Charles's sub, but this Charles suited him perfectly, more than he could have imagined on his own. He never wanted to leave him. He'd never felt happier.

Charles returned with the collar in his hand. It was the most beautiful collar he had ever seen, and it was his first one. He only hoped he was a perfect sub. Thoughts of upsetting Charles by his lack of proper behavior or making him angry worried Nathan greatly.

"You can stand now, arms behind your back, and look at me." Charles's beautiful blue eyes shone with his final approval.

"Nathan," Charles said, "I promise to protect you. I'll never violate your trust in me. This collar will be a mark of your submission to me and my oath to protect you."

He kissed Nathan's lips. He loved the taste of Charles's kisses.

"Normally, I'd mark your ass as mine, but I'm going to wait until tonight for that."

"Yes, Sir," Nathan whispered.

"I have another way to mark you now."

"Yes, Sir." Nathan wanted to play in the playroom now, but Charles couldn't help it that the police had turned up making that impossible.

Charles gestured to the bed. Nathan made his way to it, lay flat on his back, and waited for more directions. Charles undressed and stood over the bed. His erect cock was huge in every way. Nathan's eyes lit up at Charles's naked body.

"Sir, I love your big cock. I hope you'll let me show my appreciation by allowing me to take care of it."

"Turn over, young man," Charles ordered.

Nathan flipped over onto his stomach with enthusiasm. Charles put a condom on and climbed onto the bed. He pushed Nathan's legs apart and knelt between them. Charles squirted lube onto his fingers and massaged Nathan's hole. He wiggled his finger in but didn't touch his prostate. He applied more lube and pushed a second finger in, then a third, fingering Nathan fiercely.

"Like that?" Charles asked.

"Yes, Sir." Nathan's cock stood fully erect against his stomach, trapped against the bedsheets, and ready for pleasure.

Charles eased his lubed cock into Nathan's opening, then in one long, slow stroke, he pushed in. A burning pain shot through Nathan's legs, ass, and up his spine. He wasn't sure if it was from the pressure or if it took time to adjust.

With his body weight on Nathan's back and his hot breath in his ear, Charles whispered, "My cock is where it belongs. Your ass was made for me. Just relax and enjoy me."

He used the same firm but gentle voice as when he'd collared him. Nathan slowed his breathing and relaxed his ass muscles the best he could. At least he wasn't screaming in pain like the first time. Charles gave him a few more seconds to adjust before pushing his cock in and out of his ass. He slowly thrust, filling him, inch by inch, going even deeper. Every part of Nathan sang with delight. Charles stopped moving, and Nathan realized he had settled in as deep as he could go. He had given Nathan all he had, and he couldn't be happier.

"You're mine, Nathan. All mine."

"Yes, I want to be yours and only yours, Sir," Nathan panted.

Charles's cock was large any way you looked at it. He took full strokes in and out, leaving only the tip of his cock in Nathan's ass before driving back all the way in. Without any warning, Nathan tensed up, and pleasure morphed into almost unbearable pain. But just as he was going to ask Charles to stop, something amazing happened. Every time Charles drove his cock into Nathan, it punched his prostate like a hammer on a nail. Each hit sent an incredible feeling to his balls, and the pain turned to ecstasy as Charles pounded into him.

Charles slammed inside him, and his special spot ignited a fire of desire. He rocked his body and moved with Charles, who slipped his hand under Nathan and rubbed his cock. Nathan wanted this blissful feeling to last forever, but in seconds, he blasted his cum onto Charles's hand. Charles continued pumping until he came as well, spilling his cum into the condom.

"My beautiful Nathan, you feel so good."

"Hmmm." Nathan was lost in his afterglow.

"Don't move." Charles pulled out slowly, opened the drawer of the bedside table, and took out a butt plug. "You're going to wear this plug. It will hold the place for my mark for now." He inserted the plug into Nathan's ass, then fell beside Nathan and rolled him over into his arms.

"So, am I really yours now?" Nathan asked.

"Yes, you are. If you're tired, why don't you sleep a little while I go and pick up some groceries for us? If you want to go with me, you can." Charles kissed him.

"I need to sleep a little."

"Call me if you need anything."

"I will, but I'll be resting."

Charles took a shower and then left Nathan alone.

Just as he fell asleep, his phone rang.

"Hello."

"Hey, your uncle is a major suspect in your disappearance. They think he murdered you."

"Oh no. Did you tell them I'm not dead?"

"No. I don't know what to do, that's why I'm calling."

"Who do I have to call to let them know I'm fine?"

"Alma said if I know where you are, I should tell the police. I said I didn't know, but she didn't believe me."

"You can't really lie to her. She has a way of knowing when you're lying."

"I don't know what to do. The police want me at the station in an hour to discuss your whereabouts. They said they would arrest me if I don't tell them the truth."

"Damn it. Nothing is going right. Tell them I'm vacationing in Europe. Give them this number."

"Are you sure?"

"I don't want you to be arrested because I left home. Just say I'm traveling."

"I heard your uncle is furious with you for leaving. Alma said he hired some people to locate you. So be careful."

"No, you be careful. Tell them whatever you want. I'll call you when things blow over. Love you."

"Love you, too. I wish you'd come home."

"Not going to happen. Hey, I'm not a virgin anymore. I'm a sub."

"Lucky man. Finally."

After talking a little longer before finishing the call, Nathan got up, took a shower, then dressed. It seemed like Charles was gone longer than a grocery shopping trip. He decided to take a walk and think about what he should do. He didn't want to go home, but he couldn't very well let his uncle be accused of being responsible for his disappearance. One thing he didn't want was to be confronted by his uncle. The man frightened him. He had heard the stories circulating in the town about his involvement with the death of his parents. But whenever his parents were in his uncle's presence, they got along and were close to each other. He'd never believed his uncle had anything to do with their deaths. He wouldn't believe it.

Uncle Lucas refused to discuss their death, regardless of how many times Nathan had asked about it. He researched many articles on their murders. The more he read, the less he knew. Someday, he hoped he'd find out who was responsible. He wanted them punished to the fullest extent of the law for taking away his parents. He'd carried around the anger his entire life. As far as he was concerned, having to live with his uncle had ruined his life. For once in his life, he was happy with Charles.

He walked along the sand, removed his shoes, and let his feet sink into the water. It was a beautiful day. Why was his life so complicated when things were finally going his way?

He was determined to stay here with Charles. This was the right thing to do regardless, but as much as he hated his uncle, he couldn't let him pay for a crime he hadn't committed.

CHAPTER TWENTY

Charles

Charles carried the grocery bags to the kitchen. He called for Nathan when he didn't see him. He didn't answer, so maybe he was still sleeping. Charles put everything on the table, then went to the bedroom. The bed was unmade, but Nathan wasn't there. He checked the bathroom, and it was empty. Where was he? He looked for a note, but he didn't see one.

He returned to the kitchen, opened a bottle of beer, and sat down. He pulled his phone out and called Nathan. The boy better answer because Charles wasn't in the mood to lose him.

"Hi!" Nathan's cheerful voice cut the edge in Charles's mood.

"Where are you?" Charles asked, relieved to hear his voice. He could have disappeared without leaving a trace. That's all Charles needed right now. With Nathan's wild streak and habit of leaving stressful situations, anything was possible. Under Charles's watch, he'd cure him of that dangerous behavior.

"I'm testing the water behind the cottage. Why don't you come outside with me?"

Sometimes, Nathan's innocence baffled him.

"Come home." Charles ended the call. Was he going to worry each time Nathan wasn't where he should be? No wonder his uncle had made night checks. Charles figured he was overreacting from Hans's leaving. He'd have to explain to Nathan he needed to notify him of where he was going.

Within minutes, Nathan sauntered into the kitchen barefoot.

"Can I help you, Sir?" Nathan asked.

"No. But you can watch where I put things so you know where everything goes for the next time."

"Are you upset with me because I left the house without telling you?"

"You could have left a note. I expected you to be home. If you plan to leave the house, write me a note, or send a text. That's a new rule."

"I'm sorry. I'll do that next time."

Charles knew he'd made a big deal about nothing, but he had to know where Nathan was at all times. In the back of his mind, he worried Internet Charles might kidnap him for himself. He had no idea how a man played a young man like Nathan, then broke his heart or worse.

"While you were shopping, Jacob called and told me what was going on with my uncle. He's probably going to be pissed off. I don't want to see him."

"I won't let your uncle hurt you in any way. You're under my protection, not his."

"I hope so because he's pretty mean and I don't want to be around him anymore."

"You're with me. Don't worry about him."

"My uncle is under suspicion for my disappearance. What should I do?"

Charles turned around and saw the confusion in Nathan's eyes.

"You're going to have to call the police and tell them you're on vacation."

"What if they want me to return to see me in person?"

Charles noticed Nathan's hair was lighter, much lighter. He wasn't outside that long for his hair to be sun-kissed. What else was he hiding from him?

"If you have to return to prove you're you, then I'll go with you. There's no way you're going back alone. Why is your hair so light today?"

"I dyed it dark brown before I left. I have lighter hair."

"Why would you do that?"

"Charles told me to color it. He prefers darker hair."

"What kind of nutcase tells you to color your hair?"

"I just wanted to please him. Are you angry my hair isn't dark?"

Tears trickled down his cheeks indicating how he'd clearly upset Nathan with his harsh tone. Nathan was going to be a fantastic loyal sub as long as no one removed him from Charles.

"No. I just have to get used to seeing you with lighter hair. I like you either way, but don't dye your hair."

"It's not permanent hair color. It washes out with each wash."

"From here on in, ask permission before you make any changes in your appearance."

"Yes, Sir."

"I missed you. I had to cancel our horse-riding meeting with James and Tyler."

"That's too bad. I was really looking forward to it."

"We'll be able to go horseback riding another time. Let's talk about you."

"What about me, Sir?"

"If you decide to stay here with me as my sub, I want you to go to school. What do you want to study?"

"I want to study journalism. I like to write."

"Then I suggest we search for a school for you."

"I've already been accepted at the University of Pennsylvania, but I guess I won't be going there."

"Do you want to go there?"

"I want to be with you. School isn't that important right now. I could always go later."

"If you don't go to school here, you will attend UPenn."

"Are you saying you'd make me go back there to school if I don't go here?"

"Do you remember rule five?"

"Yes, Sir."

"Recite it then."

"Master Charles has the final say."

"Then what I say goes. You will go to school here because you live with me."

"Yes, Sir."

Charles made his way closer to Nathan and wrapped him in his arms.

"You're extremely important to me and I want the best for you. Do you understand?"

"Yes, Sir."

"Go to the bedroom, strip off all your clothes, and bend over the bed. I'm going to mark your ass. You need reminding who you belong to."

"Yes, Sir." He left the kitchen.

Charles's phone rang. It was James.

"Can you talk?"

"Yes. What's up?" Charles asked.

"I had a visit from Hans. He's a mess."

"Yes, he is. He tried to use his knife on Nathan this morning. I threw him out of my home."

"Well, I have a story for you. Hans received several messages that you were in the US cheating on him. They also told him you were bringing your new sub home and you were going to kick Hans out. That's why he left. He's heartbroken."

"Who told him that?"

"He said a man named David, who claimed to be your ex-partner, told him tons of things about you and your new boyfriend."

"David? Does he have a last name?" This story explained Hans's behavior. It was too bad he hadn't trusted him enough to know that story was just a lie.

"No. What are you going to do about Hans?"

"Hans left me, remember? He could have told me about this and asked if it was true. He didn't."

"So, who is David?"

"From my past."

"Do you mean your real past in Atlantic City?"

"Yes. So, he's after me. I figured he would find me, and he did."

"What about Hans?"

"I'm done with Hans. I have Nathan, and he's my new sub."

"You made him your sub?"

"That's what we both wanted."

"He doesn't have any experience in the lifestyle."

"It just so happens, he does. If you talk to Hans, tell him there is no chance for us to get back together."

"How do you know Nathan wasn't sent by David?"

"I know Nathan. I trust him and you should too." Charles ended the call.

After that call, he wasn't in the mood to play with Nathan, but he hated to let him down. He couldn't put away his worries about David. He was going to have to call his father and discuss his next move. There was no way he should flog or paddle Nathan when he was so disturbed. He went to the bedroom where Nathan waited for him bending over the bed. His sweet ass was just gorgeous, but he couldn't indulge himself when he wasn't totally calm and in control.

"Stand up and face me," Charles ordered.

Nathan followed Charles's order and faced him.

"Did you change your mind, Sir?"

"I did. Get dressed and I'm going to explain some things to you. Meet me in the kitchen."

"Yes, Sir." The disappointment in his voice hurt him. He knew Nathan saw it as a rejection.

He had made them chocolate shakes by the time Nathan entered the kitchen.

"Are you so upset with me because I left the house without telling you?"

"This has nothing to do with your actions today. There are things in my past that I'm not proud of, and I found out some upsetting news."

"Are you going to send me to the hotel?"

"No. I want you more than anything. James called while you were upstairs. He told me that whoever wants to destroy me told Hans I was cheating on him and that when I returned from the US, I would be replacing him. That's why he left me, and that's why he came at you. That doesn't give him the right to behave the way he did. He was wrong. He should have come to me and asked if it were true before he left."

"I figured it was something like that. He was enraged when he saw me in your kitchen. I knew it. So, I guess you're going to take him back now, right?"

"Wrong. I just said I want you. Hans and I hadn't been getting along for a long time. I don't want him back."

"Do you know who told Hans that story about you?"

"Someone from my past."

CHAPTER TWENTY-ONE

Nathan

James's phone call about Hans changed everything. The information about Hans had disturbed Charles enough that he no longer wanted to mark him. Unfortunately, Hans played a much larger part in Charles's heart than he'd admit, which explained the abrupt change of plans. He had to figure a way to keep Charles's attention on him and away from Hans. Nathan's wavering confidence level meant he lacked the ability to see anything positive from the new information Charles had received.

"Nathan, I need to make some phone calls. I'll be in the computer room. Don't disturb me for an hour. If you have an emergency, send me a text." Charles's frosty tone frightened Nathan.

"Yes, Sir. I'll be in here reading."

Circumstances weren't quite what he'd like them to be. He didn't think he would lose the battle for Charles initially, or was this how it was supposed to be. He had to trust Charles as his Dom. It didn't matter how he felt. He believed their relationship would have made him feel happy all the time, rather than the highs and lows he was experiencing. With all Charles's experience as a Dom, Nathan expected Charles to know that after changing his marking decision over a phone call about Hans that he would need extra attention. Instead, Charles had basically told him to buzz off for an hour. Nathan imagined him calling Hans. Within an hour, he'd know if he were out the door, and Hans would be back with Charles. He didn't know how to feel positive about the current situation. In London, Nathan had no one except Charles. What would he do if Charles told him to move out, or would he keep them both? Nathan would never accept being a second to anyone when it came to a BDSM or love relationship. He sought all Charles's love and attention. Nathan refused to share him with Hans or anyone else who might turn up from Charles's past.

As soon as Charles left him alone, he crashed on the padded chair beside the desk and felt deeply depressed, almost as if the world had ended. He was near tears, but he refused to cry over someone he hardly knew. Charles hadn't known the complete truth about his past. If anyone found out what he was doing in Philadelphia on the weekends, no one would ever want him around. Running away was the only solution to save himself from total destruction. If Uncle Lucas found out about his indiscretions with Mr. Blanken, he'd make sure Nathan never received his share of the money and the Neumann Riding Academy from his parents. Even his best friend, Jacob, didn't know about it. With all of their conversations, Jacob still didn't understand why he'd left the country. Normally, Jacob had been the one who checked his wild ideas and actions, but this time, Nathan had closed Jacob out with what he had gotten involved in. Leaving the country was the only solution he could see to end his multiplying problems. No one could ever find out.

Nathan lacked a sense of well-being most of the time, so this wasn't a new feeling. He doubted his ability to be honest, dependable, and likable. His confidence in himself dropped even lower with the rejection from the two Doms. He felt unloved and unwanted. Whenever someone he cared about disappointed him, as had happened with both men named Charles, he isolated himself. That way, he didn't have to deal with the hurt, nor would he do or say things he'd regret later. However, his current situation trapped him here with Charles, but he had no problem closing Nathan out for an hour to mend his relationship with Hans. That had to be why he didn't want Nathan to disturb him, unless he had an emergency. Charles needed only one hour to convince Hans to return to him after he explained he'd never cheated on him while he was away. All that would end well for them. Once again, Nathan was left alone. If he could find the other Charles, maybe he'd change his mind and proceed with their online agreement, but this Charles refused to let him in on who Internet Charles really was and where he could be reached.

Nathan grabbed his phone from his pocket and checked for messages. He trembled when he read the text from the man who had threatened him in the past. Despite his resolve to purge the fear of Mr. Blanken, it increased when he read the message, once again threatening the safety zone he had thought he attained by moving to another country. The man had reached him across the

Atlantic Ocean. How could he fight that reach? No place would be safe from the man.

Willem Blanken: *You have one week to return to work. I know where you are and who you're with. You signed a contract. If you choose to ignore the contract, I know where your Uncle Lucas and your friend Jacob live.*

Nathan steadied his breath and tried to calm the panic overwhelming him. The fear became tangible, immobilizing him, his daunting thoughts holding him captive. The terror from Mr. Blanken washed over his body, raising the fine hairs on the back of his neck. The sudden shock of the man he had run from threatening him once again made his muscles tense. Sweat poured down his body as he stayed as still as possible. He had to fight his fear and actively seek a solution. A feeling of dread crept up from the pit of his stomach.

Immediately, Nathan deleted the message, fearing Charles might see it, and there would be no way to explain his tattered past. No one could know the truth. He wanted to run away from everything and everyone. One day, Charles and Jacob would learn the truth and end their relationships with him. He thought he was safe in another country. He didn't know what to do about the situation. What if Mr. Blanken hurt Jacob? He had to warn him. He deserved that much, but then he'd have to tell him why he really left. To think Nathan had believed Internet Charles would solve his problems, but he only complicated them.

He left the room and walked out the back door to the beach area. He continued walking, fighting tears. He had to return and finish his time with Mr. Blanken. He owed the man the second half of the year-long contract. Why couldn't he forget about their contract? He had lied to Nathan about the details of the job. He blamed his Uncle Lucas. If he had given him the money belonging to Nathan, he wouldn't have taken the job. It looked like easy money enabling him to live on his own and away from his uncle.

He sat down on the sand with the wind blowing his hair and called Jacob.

"Hey, what's up?" Jacob asked.

"Did you meet with the police?" Nathan asked.

"Yes. They said I had to tell you to come home to prove you are alive. I told them you were going to call, but they said that wasn't good enough."

"I have a bigger problem now."

"What's wrong?"

"I hate to do this on the phone, but I have to tell you something important. There's a man in Philadelphia who employed me to work for him. I signed a contract, then left without telling him. He sent me a text, threatening me by saying he knows where you and my uncle live. He also said he knows where I am and who I am with."

"What the hell kind of job was it?" Jacob shouted.

"It's the real reason I left. I wanted to be with Charles from the gay chat. I really did, but I wouldn't have left if this man hadn't threatened me."

"Tell me what kind of job. Is this why you disappeared on the weekends without me?"

"I needed to earn money because my uncle refused to give me any of my own. He didn't pay me enough for teaching the students how to ride horses and taking care of the horses, so I could get my own place. I wanted to be free of him."

"Why won't you tell me what kind of job?"

"I just can't right now, but I will. I promise I'll tell you when I'm safe. I'm calling you to warn you to be careful when you go out. I'm sorry for putting you in danger and not telling you what I was doing. I can't tell you right now because the man threatened me if I told anyone, and I believe he will hurt me. I'm sorry, Jacob. And things with Charles are taking a bad turn. I think he's going to take back his last sub and throw me out."

"I can't believe you were doing dangerous things without telling me! We're like brothers, and you didn't trust me enough to tell me you were in trouble. Were you selling your ass for money?"

"I can't talk about it right now. I'm sorry. I wanted to tell you, but he threatened me."

"How could you work for someone who threatens you? What's wrong with you? I told you that you could live with me. I would've given you money."

"Are you pissed at me?"

"Fuck you, Nathan." Jacob ended the call.

Jacob was right, they were like brothers, and he should have told him, but Nathan feared his rejection, like the very one he had just received over the phone. He hadn't told him what he was doing, and he'd hung up on him anyway. Imagine if he'd told him the truth. Either way, Jacob was done with him and didn't want to talk to him anymore. The pain Nathan felt reminded him how he felt when he found out someone murdered his parents. The loss of them had overwhelmed him, as had losing Jacob just now. No one could replace him. They should have remained friends for life. That's what he had wanted for them. It was more difficult to leave him behind than he had thought, but now he was the one left alone. He deserved nothing less than this.

He removed his clothes until he was naked. No one was around the cove, so he wasn't worried anyone would see him. He wanted to feel the cold water to freeze out the fog of terror. He ran into the ice-cold water, and as soon as the water was high enough, he swam with one hand following the other hand dipping into the water, then above his head. Each time his arm was above the water, the cold pained him. He continued the spear motions with his arms and kicking his legs underwater. He had never been in near-freezing water. He expected he'd warm up after a while, but it got frostier.

Out of nowhere, his left leg cramped, and he tried to swim with the spasm. He couldn't use his painful leg, freezing and shaking in the water, forcing him to tread water while he tried to reach to work the painful knot in his calf. When that didn't work, he rested on his back, floating as the sharp cramp wore him out. He took a deep breath, and the freezing air went into his lungs, intensifying the spasm. He gasped as more cold air went into his lungs, and it was as if he were drowning. He flipped over to see how far away he was from the shoreline. Charles was standing on the sand removing his shoes. He ran into the water with his clothes on, swimming towards him. Within minutes, he was treading water beside Nathan.

"What happened?" Charles asked, breathing hard.

"I got a cramp. I couldn't move my leg."

"Get on my back, and I'll carry you back to the shore."

Nathan sighed in relief, resting his head on Charles's shoulder. Charles was breathing hard and fast. Maybe going for a swim wasn't one of his best ideas to feel better. His stupid adolescent actions made his problems worse. But then, Nathan knew he was the world's worst problem solver. He lacked the skills to work things out to his advantage.

"We don't swim alone here and never naked," Charles said.

"It was so damn cold. I thought I would be okay, but the water was way too cold."

Charles swam faster than he had imagined. Before he knew it, they were on the sand. Charles helped him get his clothes back on, picked up his own shoes, then helped him back to the cottage.

"I'm sorry. I'm sorry you had to swim out to help me."

"You're in big trouble with me." Charles opened the door for them.

Nathan knew he had broken a rule to let Charles know if he was leaving the house. His distress and confusion caused him to ignore any rules. He didn't care since he thought Charles wanted Hans back. Charles was way too smart to admit it, but Nathan felt the cold distance from him. One damn phone call had broken their connection. *We're over. Just tell me.*

"Let's take a hot shower and warm up." Charles mussed Nathan's hair.

Charles said nothing about his phone calls. This was yet another silent declaration Nathan was on his way out.

CHAPTER TWENTY-TWO

Charles

Charles helped remove Nathan's clothes and turned on the warm water in the shower. He was icy cold and looked terribly ill. His lips turned blue.

"Stand under the hot water," Charles ordered as he removed his clothes. He stepped into the stall with Nathan.

"I'm still cold," Nathan trembled.

Charles got out of the shower and grabbed two large towels. He dried himself first, then he threw his towel into the hamper.

"Get out of there so I can dry you." He turned off the water, then held another towel for him.

Nathan dillydallied out of the stall. Charles wrapped him in the towel and put another one around his wet hair. He helped him to the bedroom and into the bed.

"Stay under the covers. I'm going to get more covers, then make you something hot. Don't get out of this bed for any reason."

Nathan nodded as if he had no energy to answer with his voice. Charles collected two extra heavy blankets and put them over the covers. He found sweats and slipped them under the covers for Nathan.

"Put these on. I'll be right back." Charles left the room, raced to the kitchen, and made some hot chocolate for him. Once the milk and chocolate finished cooking, he returned to the bedroom. Nathan was still quivering, unable to warm up, and he looked ghastly.

"This is hot, so let me hold the mug, and you sip slowly."

Again, Nathan nodded but didn't say anything. However, Charles noticed he wore the sweats.

"How do you feel?"

"Cold."

"Why did you decide to swim naked in the sea? You never swim anywhere without a lifeguard or a buddy. You could have drowned. Don't ever go swimming without my permission. And I didn't see any notes or texts from you."

"I left because I was upset."

"About what?" Charles couldn't believe his ears. Why would he be upset?

"I don't know what kind of Dom you are, but you shut me down for an hour to call your ex-sub, and you think it's okay to do that to me after you canceled my marking."

Nathan's eyes appeared to have a film of glass over them. The same way they had looked after talking to that man in the hotel lobby. Clearly, he had been upset when Charles told him not to disturb him. He hadn't thought that stopping the marking and making private phone calls would upset him. Nathan had attached his own interpretation on why he hadn't marked him. He needed to learn more about the lifestyle. James had been right, Nathan lacked experience, and his so-called virtual BDSM relationship was another lie to garner what he had wanted.

"Do your eyes hurt?"

"Yes, I got saltwater in them." He looked away, breaking eye-contact.

"I've seen your eyes look red and glassy before. Maybe I should take you to see an ophthalmologist."

"No. I don't need to see a doctor. I wear contacts, and sometimes, they make my eyes red and teary looking."

"I never saw you remove or clean your lenses at night."

"Sometimes, I take them off in the middle of the night."

"Why is that?"

"Because I didn't want you to know."

"This isn't making any sense, Nathan. What are you hiding?"

"The other Charles told me he wanted a guy with dark hair and eyes. So, I got the contacts and since you met me with them on, I thought I'd better keep them in when you were around. I was afraid you wouldn't like my real eye color."

Charles got up and pulled a hand mirror out of the bathroom cabinet drawer. He got two washcloths, one with soap and the other one with water. He returned to the bedroom and washed Nathan's hands, then rinsed them with the other washcloth.

"Remove those contacts. I'm going to throw them away."

"Yes, Sir," Nathan whispered.

Nathan pulled down his lower eyelid, carefully pinched the contact off, then looked up and slid the lens down. His brown eyes turned to a brilliant electric blue. Why would he change his appearance to this degree? Internet Charles hadn't shown up, so why maintain the disguise? Maybe because he still believed he was really Internet Charles.

He removed the other one then handed them to Charles.

"My eyes really hurt."

"You have beautiful eyes. I don't understand why you continued wearing them with me. I never told you what you should or shouldn't look like. I don't understand why you're disguising yourself. Why did you do this after you knew the other Charles was out of the picture?"

"I thought you might have had the same preferences as that Charles."

"That's a lie! After you saw Hans, why would you think that?" Charles didn't appreciate Nathan lying to him. He wasn't buying his reasons for wearing the contacts.

"I don't know."

"You know, and you're lying to me."

"I'm sorry."

Charles went to the bathroom, threw the lenses into the trashcan, then found some eye drops for his red eyes. Nathan looked like a completely different person. Charles didn't buy the reasons he gave for continuing the charade. If this wasn't a red flag, then what was? He'd get to the bottom of this, but he still didn't believe Nathan was part of the setup. He behaved as if he were hiding or running away from someone. He'd committed himself as a Dom to Nathan, regardless of his past; he wanted him, regardless if he had committed some unforgivable sin. Of course, he knew he couldn't change him completely, but he planned on making him respect himself first. He lied for a reason. Charles wanted to know why, and he'd find out one way or another.

"You earned your first punishment, which will be administered tomorrow, if you're well enough."

"I should have left a note, but I was upset."

"I told you I don't want Hans back in my life. You have no reason to be upset when I needed an hour away from you to make phone calls. I didn't mark you for a reason, and not the reason you've manufactured in your head. Understand that as a Dom, I have to be one hundred percent with you when I mark you. My mind must be free of all things. After the phone call, I was disturbed to hear someone from my past was causing problems."

"Are you going to tell me who is causing you problems? Did he pretend to be you?"

"Are you feeling warmer?"

"Yes, Sir." Nathan rolled his eyes.

"This is your one and only warning. Don't roll your eyes when I'm speaking to you. It's a sign of disrespect and worthy of serious punishment."

"Yes, Sir. That won't be repeated."

"That's a wise decision on your part. I'm not going to tell you who yet. I must make sure it was him. It looks like it might be a man I knew years ago." Charles had no intention of informing Nathan about David. His past didn't need to resurface.

"Did you call Hans, Sir?"

"They were private phone calls. If I wanted you to know who I called, you could've sat in my office while I made them."

"I see."

"Are you sure you feel warmer?"

"I'm fine. Don't worry about me. I didn't know the water was so cold here."

"Do you like Chinese food?"

"I'm not hungry. I want to go to sleep."

"If you get hungry, let me know, and I'll call out for something. I'll let you rest." Charles kissed Nathan.

Charles left Nathan and went to his office again. His phone rang. His annoyance increased and he clenched his jaw when he saw it was Hans calling. Breaking up with Hans wasn't painful, even though Hans initiated it based on a lie. The reasons for accepting Hans ending their relationship were far too numerous to count. Yes, Hans was adorable and an excellent sub. If only he'd had deeper feelings for him. He couldn't manufacture them, however, regardless of how hard he had tried. That was the basis of why they didn't and couldn't ever work out as a long-term couple. It would be best if Hans found someone else who didn't have to work so hard to love him. Charles answered his cell. "What do you want, Hans?"

"I'm calling to warn you about Nathan Neumann."

"How can you warn me about a person you don't know?" Charles shook his head in disbelief.

"I know about him, and you should too. He works for a shady guy in Philadelphia. I'm positive he was sent here to destroy you, and he will if you don't dump him."

"What are you talking about?"

"I'm talking about a Dutch criminal named Willem Blanken. He's from the Netherlands but relocated to Philadelphia to continue his shady businesses. Your precious boy works for him."

"How did you come by this information?"

"The same man who told me you were cheating on me while you were in the US. He was right because you did bring home another sub. I wonder what you would have done if I hadn't left."

"I'm going to say this once, and only once. You left me. If you're so stupid to believe what this guy is telling you, then you'd better go back home and live with your parents to stay safe. If you continue to interfere in my relationship with Nathan, I'll have you deported." Charles ended the call.

So, this person not only wanted to destroy him, but he wanted to hurt Nathan, too. He wasn't sure how all this meshed, but it was time to call his father. Charles would look up this Willem Blanken. Nathan would have to answer to him if he were part of setting him up to lose his job. He wasn't looking forward to talking to his father. He was the only one who would be able to solve the problem. He tapped his father's number.

"Charles, how nice that you called me."

"I have a problem, and I need your help."

"What's wrong?"

"David has located where I am. I believe he is setting me up to get fired from my job."

"David? From Atlantic City?"

"Yes, I think he's the one who is working to destroy me."

"What has he done?"

"He impersonated me and went into a gay chat room. He got involved with minors and other young men. He was able to use my ISP address and sent the information to the board where I work. They are currently investigating me, and I'm on a leave of absence."

"I'm going to pull some strings and see what I can find out. It's not right. You made one fucking mistake, and now you're supposed to be indebted to them for the rest of your life? Stay calm. I'm going to take care of this."

"Thank you. That means a lot to me."

"You know I want you to move back home. Your mother hates you living in London."

"I know, but I moved because I was supposed to be safe and away from David."

"You weren't far enough from him and his friends. Don't worry. This too will be handled."

"I want you to know I'm living with a young man from Pennsylvania."

"What happened to the Dutch boy?"

"He left."

"Where exactly in Pennsylvania is this new boy from?"

"Chadds Ford. He's Lucas Neumann's nephew."

"Interesting."

"I need you to do a check on him and a man named Willem Blanken. Can you do that for me?"

"What's Neumann's nephew's name?"

"Nathaniel Neumann, but he goes by Nathan. I want to make sure he's not in any trouble with Willem Blanken."

"I feel for Nathan. No one likes Lucas for a reason. Take care of that boy."

"I had good parents, and I still fucked up big time."

"You turned out okay because you turned around and made something of yourself. Your mistakes are your past, and soon it will be over for good."

"Tell Mom I love her."

"I will. I'll call when I have more information. Stay safe."

CHAPTER TWENTY-THREE

Nathan

Nathan got up to look for Charles. His sweats were too large, so he rolled the legs and arms. Nothing was going the way he wanted it to. What was he going to do about Jacob? When he found Charles preparing dinner in the kitchen, he wondered what he'd been doing while Nathan was sleeping.

"What are you cooking, Sir?"

"I'm marinating steak and making a salad for dinner. I see you are okay now."

"I'm hungry, really hungry. Can I help make the salad?"

"Sit down and relax. I'll take care of it. After dinner we're going to talk about your behavior. I'm not happy with you ignoring my rules. Regardless of your feelings, rules are to be obeyed."

"I'm sorry, Sir. I knew I was supposed to leave you a note or send you a message."

"Then it was deliberate, wasn't it?"

"Yes, Sir. I wanted to leave without notifying you."

"Leave the house or leave me?"

"At the time, both. I want to be your sub, but I was convinced you were going to ask me to leave after that phone call."

"You earned yourself your first punishment, but that won't be implemented until tomorrow. Tonight, after dinner, we're going to just relax and talk."

"I just want you to know something about me."

"I'm listening." Charles turned around to face him.

"Under no circumstances will I ever share you with anyone else."

Charles moved closer to Nathan. "I promise you that taking on another sub is the furthest thought from my mind. I only want you. I'm not into threesomes."

"Have you ever done a threesome?"

"No." Charles returned to the counter and chopped up the vegetables for the salad.

Nathan hoped Charles meant what he said, but regardless, he was positive Hans could convince Charles to take him back. How did he explain stopping the marking over a phone call about Hans? He didn't.

Charles filled their plates with steak and a bowl with the salad, then put them on the table.

Nathan cut his meat and tasted a piece. "It tastes delicious."

"Thank you. How do your eyes feel?"

"Much better. I'm glad I don't have to wear them."

"You have beautiful eyes. Are you sure you aren't hiding from someone?"

"I'm not hiding except I don't want my uncle to know I'm here, but I guess I'm going to have to return to prove he didn't hurt me in any way."

"I need to take a trip to Philadelphia, so we can combine our trips."

"Why Philadelphia?" Nathan grimaced.

"I have business there."

"What kind of business, Sir?"

"I'm a major investor in properties there and I need to sell one. I got a good offer, so I need to negotiate a price in person with the potential buyers."

"Will we stay in Philadelphia?" Nathan didn't buy Charles had to meet with investors. Certainly, Charles was aware of the internet. He must have another reason for wanting to make this trip. He was just there.

"Yes. Do you have a problem with staying in Philadelphia?"

"No problem, Sir."

"Good. Then we'll take care of the police business, and you can visit your friend Jacob."

"I don't know if he wants to see me anymore."

"Why not?"

"We had a disagreement. He's angry with me because I didn't tell him every detail of my life."

"When people are close, they share the details with each other. I suppose he was hurt, especially since you left Chadds Ford."

"When are we going to leave for Philadelphia?" Nathan asked. Charles had no problem leaving him out of who he had called and who that person was from the past.

"As soon as I can book us a flight."

"I guess that's the right thing to do."

"Yes, we'll take care of your disappearance issue for your uncle. Do you want to see him?"

"No. Never if I can help it."

"Let's go outside and sit."

THE NEXT DAY, NATHAN woke up in an empty bed. Charles's voice could be heard in the hallway. He wondered who he was shouting at. Nathan got out of bed and took a quick shower, then dressed. When he stepped into the kitchen, he found Charles there pacing back and forth.

"Good morning, Sir."

"Good morning. Did I wake you up?"

"I heard you yelling in the hallway."

"Did you hear what I was saying?"

"No, Sir. I took a shower."

"It was a phone call from the academy. They dismissed me. Do you know why?"

"No. I hope it's not because of me." Nathan feared their relationship would come to an end if it had to do with him.

"No. They said the case against me in regard to the chat room had insufficient evidence, but they decided to fire me because I'm gay."

"Can't you take them to court?"

"No. They are a private institution. Nothing is going the way I had envisioned. There is no reason why I can't move."

"Can we move here?"

"I'm going to check out some job opportunities in Philadelphia first, then I'll make my decision. You could go to school if we move to Philadelphia."

"I like it here away from my uncle."

"No decisions have been made."

"Are you going to mark me?"

"You are due a punishment today, so I can't mark you on the same day. We'll put it off until you heal from it."

"What kind of punishment?" Once again, Charles pushed his marking away for another reason. This time it was his punishment. Surely, he could mark and discipline at the same time? Maybe Doms weren't allowed to change that order, or Charles believed discipline came before the marking. Nathan questioned whether Charles really wanted to mark him.

"We're going back home today. So, I'm going to punish you on the spanking bench. I haven't decided with what implement yet. I can assure you the punishment will fit the transgressions."

"Are you still angry at me?" Nathan detected a change in Charles's tone again. He could say whatever he wanted, but his smug attitude sucked. For some reason, he wouldn't admit he was angry. *There were no angry Doms because they were perfect at all times.* Charles thought he was above common human emotions. No wonder Hans walked out on him without telling him in advance.

"I'm disappointed in your behavior and your lack of trust in me. I'm not your enemy."

"I know that, but you keep important things from me."

"Like what?" His brows drew together in an angry frown.

Nathan feared awakening Charles's temper like the one he'd displayed with Hans. He swore he wouldn't tolerate another angry person in his life. Living with Uncle Lucas and working for Mr. Blanken were more than he could handle in one lifetime, and he shouldn't have to either. Charles needed to calm down before Nathan walked away from everything they had, the good and the bad.

"Like the guy from your past, who is causing your problems. I'd like to know if he was the same person who pretended to be you in the chat room."

"Do you prefer your Internet Charles to me?" Charles had a habit of ignoring Nathan's questions by asking a question.

"I want to know why he led me on, and why he didn't pick me up at the airport."

"You didn't answer my question." Charles's jaw clenched and his eyes narrowed with displeasure.

"And, Sir, you didn't answer my question either. I'm still waiting for you to name the man who was from your past."

"You're building up swats with your insolent attitude. Don't speak to me in that offensive manner." Charles sent him a threatening glare.

Nathan opened his mouth to say something mean and insulting, but he stopped himself when the image of Charles throwing Hans out of his home appeared in his mind. He didn't want Charles to treat him like that, so he tempered his remarks. He had enough problems and needed Charles on his side, not as an enemy.

"I don't understand, Sir. Why are you ignoring my questions when it involves me?"

"If you were paying attention to our previous conversation concerning this topic, I said I didn't know for sure. I also told you I'll inform you who it was when I'm certain who it was."

"I heard you the first time, Sir. But you must have believed that person from your past had a hand in this mess because you reacted like you were too upset to mark me."

"Your punishment is increasing by the moment. I'm not going to mark you, but I'm going to punish you, right now. Go to the bedroom and prepare for your discipline." He glared at Nathan with burning, reproachful eyes.

Nathan stood. "And how should I prepare myself, Sir?" Nathan heard the bratty tone in his voice. He was losing patience with Charles. His problems from his past landed the man on a hate mission. So, he was okay to punish him, but not mark him. He didn't know if he was still his sub.

"Remove your clothes and bend over the bed. Knock off the rebellious tone. You'll learn to respect me." There was a tinge of coldness in his voice.

"Yes, Sir." Nathan lowered his voice, being purposely remorseful. He spun around and made his way to the bedroom. He had plenty to learn when it came to a proper, respectful response to Charles's corrections. His uncle often told him his attitude needed adjustment. Some of his teachers had complained he had spoken to them without any respect. More than once a teacher had called his uncle about his disrespectful behavior in class. He must figure out a way to adjust his insolent attitude, even if he didn't mean it.

Nathan removed his clothes, which he didn't want to do. However, he had no choice in the matter at this point since he'd agreed to accept his punishment.

He was completely naked when he bent over the bed. This wasn't how he thought the beginning of their relationship would turn out. He wanted Charles to mark him before his first punishment. This wasn't going to be fun at all. He looked over to the doorway and Charles appeared with a belt in his hand. The blood began to pound in his temples. Anger and sadness set his mood; Nathan had failed when he should have been on a high from Charles marking him.

"I'm going to give you ten swats with my belt. Use your safeword if you want me to stop."

"Yes, Sir," Nathan said with hope Charles would lower the number of swats. He wanted to negotiate the number of swats, but one of the rules said to accept his punishment. He was in enough trouble with mouthing off to him. Charles would never accept his part in causing Nathan to display disrespect.

Charles stepped to the side of the bed. "Why are you getting punished?"

"I didn't leave you a note or a text when I left, and I talked back to you."

"Five swats are for not notifying me where you were going. The other five for being disrespectful to me. I ought to add another ten for you swimming naked and alone in the sea, but it's your first punishment, so I'll go easy on you this time."

Charles whirled the belt in the air causing the hairs on his body to stand up. Nathan wished he would have shut the hell up or taken his anger out when he was alone. He'd better learn to shut his mouth around Charles. He meant business when he disciplined.

The first strike against his ass bit him. He pulled the comforter up with the hope of avoiding the blows, but to no avail. The second, third, fourth, and fifth swats whipped him like millions of bees stinging. He needed to get to ten.

"This hurts!" Nathan said.

"It's meant to hurt. You're being punished." Charles continued whipping him with the belt.

By now, Nathan lost count of the swats, wiggling, and whimpering to avoid the whipping, but nothing stopped the belt from meeting his backside. Charles whipped with a definite pattern, beginning on the upper part of his ass, and striking the belt down to his upper thighs.

Nathan bit his lip to prevent himself from screaming every time the belt struck him. Tears poured down his cheeks. His cock remained erect for reasons

Nathan didn't understand. The pain Charles was inflicting brought his cock pleasure.

"I hope this teaches you an important lesson. Notify me when you leave and speak to me with respect at all times!"

"I promise it won't happen again, Sir," Nathan promised, not knowing if he could control his feelings when he was angry with Charles.

When he was done, Charles rubbed some cream on Nathan's ass, easing the stinging.

CHAPTER TWENTY-FOUR

Charles

After dinner, Charles directed Nathan to read an article online about the role of a sub. The boy knew less than he had first thought. He went outside for privacy when his phone buzzed. The message was from Hans. When he opened it up, there were several attached still photos of Nathan without clothes in various poses. The background appeared to be a room with a bed. He pinched the picture larger to see if there was anything to indicate it was Nathan's bedroom, but he couldn't see any personal articles giving away who the room belonged to. The steel blue bedroom was huge. That seemed strange for some reason, even though he didn't know Nathan's favorite color. Several explicit images revealed Nathan performing a striptease, masturbating onto the floor, and posing in erotic positions. How did Hans get these?

He'd never had a situation resembling this one with any subs or boyfriends. How would Nathan explain these photos? Were they on the internet? His feelings veered from nausea to anger. Maybe Hans had set Nathan up. He had good reason after he discovered Nathan sitting in his chair. Nathan had acted so innocent, and he was alone in those pictures. He could have posed virtually without physically connecting to a man. Nathan claimed he was a virgin unless he was going for an Academy Award for his convincing acting skills. No one had ever conned Charles, and he doubted Nathan was street smart enough to do so, but he couldn't explain these incriminating photos.

He made reservations to Philadelphia, then found Nathan.

"What did you think of the BDSM article?"

"I guess having a real relationship is far different from having one online. I'm sorry for leaving without telling you," Nathan explained.

"Are you sorry about being disrespectful to me?"

"Yes, Sir. It won't happen again."

"We're leaving in the morning, so we need to drive back to the house and pack. We don't have enough here. Can you be ready in ten minutes?"

"Yes, Sir."

"Get used to being punished severely for breaking rules. Pay attention to how you respond to me and above all, follow the rules."

"I learned that today, Sir."

Nathan's phone buzzed. He saw it was a text from Jacob.

"Who is that from?"

"Jacob."

"Answer it." Charles stood behind Nathan and read the texts as he typed them.

Jacob: *Your uncle is in jail. Sorry about hanging up, but you should have told me.*

Nathan: *In jail? Why? We're flying out tomorrow. Can we meet?*

Jacob: *They arrested your uncle for shooting someone on his property. He claims it was self-defense. You better come and see me.*

Nathan: *Are they keeping him or letting him out on bail?*

Jacob: *Alma said he has a hearing in the morning, and she thinks he'll be out.*

Nathan: *I'll call you when I'm in Chadds Ford.*

Jacob: *I love you. Take care.*

Nathan: *I love you too. See you soon.*

"I'm glad you heard back from Jacob. You need him in your life. I'd love to meet him, but I want you to spend some time with him alone too."

"Thanks."

"We both have friends from our past and should not neglect them."

"When are you going to mark me?"

"Soon. You must heal from your punishment. Regardless, you're still my sub, in case you think you're not." Charles took Nathan in his arms. "You're even hotter with your own color hair and eyes."

"So, you like the real me?"

"I love the real you. Let's start back."

AS SOON AS THEY LANDED in Philadelphia, Charles rented a red sports car and drove them to the hotel. Charles had called the Chadds Ford Police Department and made an appointment for Nathan to discuss his disappearance. Saying Nathan was anxious to talk to the police was an understatement. What he needed was support and encouragement. Nathan feared his uncle, which Charles understood having met the man. Everyone knew him in Chadds Ford, but no one liked him. They ignored him or tolerated his nasty personality, only engaging when necessary.

When they entered the police department, Charles walked alongside Nathan to the counter. They asked Charles to wait outside while they questioned Nathan in a private room down the hallway behind the service desk. After thirty minutes, Nathan came out, looking a bit nervous but relieved.

"I'm all done. They cleared him on my disappearance. He might be out on bail by tonight for the other matter."

"Do you want to see Jacob?"

"Yes. I'd like that."

"Where does he live?"

"On Oak Avenue. Are you driving me there now?"

"Yes. Send him a text. I have an appointment with the investors. I'll pick you up at seven."

When they arrived at Jacob's house, Charles got out of the car with Nathan. Jacob ran to Nathan and hugged him. Nathan needed Jacob as a close friend.

"Jacob, this is Charles Moore."

"Nice to meet you," Jacob said.

"Nice to meet you too. I'll be picking Nathan up at seven."

Charles left them alone and drove back to Philadelphia. He sent a text to his father that he was in town and wanted to meet at O'Hara's. When he arrived at the restaurant, he immediately saw his father sitting in a booth. He was different from all the others. He was handsome, but not in the conventional sense. He had an appearance that made him stand out in any crowd. He was tan, from vacationing at various Pacific Islands. His bright blue eyes contrasted exceptionally well with his tan. As soon as he recognized Charles, he smiled and stood. Often, Charles could see a hint of pain in his sparkling eyes, which would disappear as suddenly as it had appeared.

His father hugged Charles. "It's good to see you again and so soon from your last visit. I have news for you and I ordered us drinks," he said as they sat.

"Thanks."

"Your mother will be disappointed she missed you. She left this morning for Bali."

"And you stayed home?"

"I've been working on your issues with David and Mr. Blanken."

"And?"

"A strong message has been sent to David. I doubt he'll bother you or Nathan again."

"What did you do?"

"I sent a message, and that's all you need to know. I'm proud of your accomplishments, and I'm sorry my reach doesn't extend to London to save your headmaster position."

"You've done more than enough for me."

"I have an offer for you. There's an opening at UPenn for a full-time English professor. Since your doctorate is in English and with your background in London, you'd fit right in. Someone owes me a favor. All you need to do is go to the interview and be who you are."

"I do need a job, and Nathan has been accepted there next semester." Charles wondered how so many coincidences surrounded his father. He seemed to manufacture solutions for him on demand when needed. How would he even know about the availability of this particular position?

"Since you're visiting, do you want me to set up an interview this week?"

"Yes and thank you for always looking after me."

"You can stay with us until you find somewhere to live."

"Thanks, but no. I need my privacy, as you know. Tell me what you found out about Mr. Blanken."

"Interesting man. Basically, he is a low-level pimp who is trafficking young people to Europe. I don't know how Nathan got involved with him. I would keep an eye on him."

"Most likely, he lied to Nathan about a job. He's young and didn't realize what he was getting into."

"You got into trouble because you were looking for a high. Why do you think Nathan fell prey to Blanken?"

"He wasn't allowed to be who he was around his uncle. He needed freedom, and he desperately needs love and care. He has such a low self-image."

"I still think Lucas had his hand in the deaths of Nathan's parents. He moved into their home so fast that their bodies hadn't even been transferred to the morgue."

"Nathan never said he thought his uncle had a part in it. I think Lucas made him feel unwanted and unloved."

"Lucas wants Nathan's share. Be careful Lucas doesn't come after you."

"He's in jail right now. He shot a trespasser on his property."

"See, he's dangerous. I hope they keep him there."

"With his money, he'll be out and will beat the charge."

"I'll send you a text when I have the date and time for the interview."

"Thanks, Dad."

Within fifteen minutes, while they were still sitting across from each other in the booth, his father sent him a text message that his interview was at ten the next morning. He was sitting across from him, but he sent him a text.

Charles looked up from his phone and said, "Thanks, Dad. That was fast."

CHAPTER TWENTY-FIVE

Nathan

Nathan and Jacob sat outside on the patio. Jacob's mother came out and brought them lemonade, both their favorite. She always treated Nathan as a second son.

"I'm happy to see you're back. Are you staying?" she asked.

"I don't know yet," Nathan said.

"You need to go to school. Don't give your life up for a man you barely know."

"He wants me in school, so I'll be going to UPenn or somewhere over there."

"Are you going to give up your citizenship?" She looked horrified because she was the mayor of Chadds Ford.

"I haven't thought about it."

"Well, it's something you need to think about." She left them and returned to the kitchen.

"I wish you weren't going back," Jacob said, pushing his dark hair out of his hazel eyes.

"Charles said we might move here if he gets a job. He lost his other one because he's gay. Someone set him up. The same person who I thought wanted me and paid for my ticket." Nathan paused. "But he won't tell me who it is."

"Why not?"

"I don't know. He said he didn't know for sure."

"Did it ever cross your mind that this Charles was the same one in the chat?"

"It has, and you know what, I don't care. I want him."

"Then why do you think he doesn't want you to know?"

"I don't know. He's secretive. I think he believes I'll confront him, then leave."

"Granted, he's hot, but can you trust him?"

"I trust he wants the best for me, and I believe he cares about me."

"Why didn't he take you to his business meeting then?"

"I don't know. Never thought about it. He wanted me to spend time with you."

"So, are you going to tell me about your job?"

"Oh, I'm not proud of that mess I made. This guy met me at a bar in Philadelphia. He offered me a job as a model. At first, they took pictures of me in all these theme outfits, like a gangster, cowboy, businessman, college student, and sportsman. Then one day, he wanted me to strip to a song. He offered me five hundred to do it. So, I did."

"That's when you should have said no."

"It gets worse. The money was good, and I kept telling myself, as soon as I get enough money to move out, I'll quit."

"And how did it get worse?"

"He took pictures of me naked and posted a page on the internet. That's where Internet Charles must have found me. I told him about my work situation. He offered to take me away from Mr. Blanken, my boss. All I had to do was become his sub and live with him in London. So, I took the deal to get away from my uncle and Mr. Blanken."

"Does this Charles know that part?"

"I didn't tell him, but I think he found out somehow. Why, all of a sudden, would he want to do business in Philadelphia? He has a nice cottage by the sea. I wish we could move there."

"You don't know him that well to isolate yourself in another country. We're supposed to go to UPenn together. Don't you want to go anymore?"

"A part of me does, and the other part wants to stay in London. I'm so mixed up with what I want. If I stay, Mr. Blanken will find me. I'll have to work until my contract is up. I bet, even then, he won't let me go."

"I think you should tell Charles. If he's your Dom then he must know so he can help you."

"But he might walk away from me."

"It's not fair to him either. He needs to be in a relationship with someone who trusts him with everything. How can he protect you? That's part of what a Dom does."

"I'll think about it. I know that's the right thing to do. The other Charles had known about it, and that's why he wanted me over there, so he could protect me. But this Charles might feel our relationship was built on lies and walk away."

"Trust him with the truth. No one can fault you for being sucked into it by a con man. If he dumps you, then you can stay here until school begins."

"I'm going to try to tell him tonight. Be on standby for my call. If he's going to dump me, it would be better here where I have you and friends."

"I bought my books for my classes. Do you want to see them?"

"Yes, we're taking the same classes. I need to get mine if we stay here."

After they checked out the textbooks and had snacks, Nathan received a text that Charles was waiting outside for him. They said their goodbyes and Nathan climbed into the red sports car with Charles behind the wheel. He must have rented another one because it wasn't the same car he'd rented at the airport.

"Why did you change cars?"

"My father lent it to me."

"Nice car."

"Did you have a good visit with Jacob?"

"I did. He showed me his textbooks for UPenn. We were taking the same classes."

"You still might be able to go there. I'm going to have an interview for a job before we go back."

"You found another job already?" Nathan had mixed feelings about returning. He wanted to go to school, but he didn't want to live near his uncle. He missed his third story part of the house, and he really missed Alma and the horses. The home should be his. He wondered if there was a way to get his uncle out of the house since it had belonged to his parents originally.

"My father found it. I met with him today."

"What about the investors?"

"I decided not to sell and canceled the meeting."

Nathan hadn't believed Charles's story about meeting with investors when he'd first told him. And now, he had a job interview. Just like that, Charles had decided to move back without blinking an eye or asking Nathan how he felt about it. Although after seeing Jacob's textbooks, he had to admit his excitement had grown substantially about the courses they had signed up for.

"You're very quiet. Did your visit go well?"

"Yes. It did. I guess everything is moving too fast."

"Am I part of everything?" Charles glanced his way.

"I don't think we're moving too fast. I like being your sub. I want this more than anything."

"That's good. I don't want you feeling pressured. Tomorrow, I'm going to mark you."

"I want that so much."

After driving for forty minutes, Charles stopped at the hotel. They took the elevator to their floor.

"I need to talk to you about something very important," Nathan said.

Charles pulled two beers out from the refrigerator. He handed one to Nathan.

"I know you're not old enough to drink in the States, but you look like you need one."

Nathan forced a smile and twisted the cap from the bottle of beer. "Thanks. I do need it."

After they removed their shoes and socks, they sat on the bed, side by side.

"Don't be afraid to tell me anything."

"I wasn't totally honest about Charles," Nathan said.

"What part wasn't?" Charles asked, kissing his cheek.

"I was desperate to leave home and live on my own. I got a job in Philadelphia. I was modeling for a gay online website and magazine. All I had to do was dress up in various outfits. I was paid a lot of money. I didn't mind my boss's plan to use my photos on a website for gay men who wanted to chat with me. It was a good way for me to meet men and make money."

"And you met Charles?" He placed his hand on Nathan's knee.

"Yes. But before I met him, I chatted with many other men. I never saw any of them in person. It was just men paying to see me and chat. I signed a contract for a year to model and place my pictures on the website. All I had to do was dress up in a few different outfits in front of the camera and chat with the men. That was in the contract I signed."

"Why did you need money when you're part-owner of the Neumann's Riding Academy?"

"That's the thing. I can't access my money or make any decisions until I'm twenty-one. My uncle didn't pay me much for working for him. He never bought anything for me except food and provided shelter. I had to use my own money from working, even when I was a kid. I just wanted to get away from him."

"Is that all?"

"No. My boss changed the terms of the contract. He wanted me to strip in front of the camera. I did that and some other things to turn men on, but I still had no physical contact with anyone. Then this man named Charles saw me on there. He asked if we could chat in a private chat room. I did. We had an online relationship, but meanwhile, my boss forced me to strip for the men online. But that wasn't all. He wanted to rent me out for the night with men. He was willing to pay me a lot of money, but I refused. He threatened to beat me up and tell my uncle what I was doing. So, I told Charles what was going on, and he sent me a ticket with strings, of course. He wanted me to be his sub. I had to live with him. So, I agreed."

"I'm sorry you were conned into that job. Why didn't you tell me until now?"

"I was afraid you would send me away and not understand what an idiot I was for doing shit like that and not figuring out how to get out of it. I was afraid to come here because he might force me to finish out my contract and tell my uncle."

"I collared you, which means you belong to me. My job is to protect you, so I'm not going to end our relationship because you were conned into a shameful job. Anyway, I'm already taking care of this situation. You don't need to know the details, only that I'm taking care of it."

"How could you be taking care of it when I just told you about it?" Nathan felt the hairs on his arms and legs stand up. His heart skipped a beat as he sat rooted to the bed.

"I knew about it before you told me, and I figured you'd tell me when you were ready."

Tears pushed through and hit his cheeks. Regardless, he didn't want to show how emotional he was over Charles's words. He had known all this time and was actively protecting him. No one ever cared enough to protect him.

"I have no words to say how much this means to me." Nathan fisted his tears away.

"Things are going to work out for us because I'm going to make sure no one takes advantage of you."

"How did you find out?"

"Hans told me."

"He looked me up and tried to make you kick me out?"

"I don't know how he found out, but I'm glad I knew because as soon as he told me, I started to work on it. That's why we're really in Philadelphia. And now, since I don't have a job in London, we're going to live near the University of Pennsylvania."

"I'm so afraid of Mr. Blanken. I might need a bodyguard."

"You have me. Mr. Blanken will be deported to the Netherlands where he belongs."

"Hans knew his name?"

"I guess Hans did an intense search, but he had help. Whoever wanted to ruin me, helped him try to hurt you and break us apart."

"Hans hates me that much?"

"I'm disappointed in him in so many ways, but our relationship had run its course."

"I hope our relationship doesn't run its course."

"Trust in me, and it won't. I want the best for you."

"I can see that now."

CHAPTER TWENTY-SIX

Nathan

Charles had promised to mark him tonight. He couldn't do it in the hotel, but knowing Charles, he'd figure something out. He couldn't imagine where though, and what would he use to mark him when he hadn't packed the implements from his playroom? Nathan was excited for them to seal their relationship. Charles was making phone calls in another room, so he couldn't hear what he was planning.

Nathan decided to send Alma a message. He had missed all her love and care. So many times, she protected him from the brunt of his uncle's fury. She was more of a relative to him than Uncle Lucas had been. Nathan loved her and hoped his not telling her where, when, or why he left home didn't hurt their relationship.

Nathan: *I'm in Philadelphia and I wish I could see you.*

Alma: *How could you leave home without telling me where you were going? Come home where you belong. Your uncle has been under a great deal of stress with the police and your disappearance. He loves you very much and was quite upset.*

Nathan: *I talked to the police so they would let up on Uncle Lucas.*

Alma: *We raised you. Why would you leave when you have everything here? Come home.*

Nathan: *Is Uncle Lucas home now?*

Alma: *No. He won't be home for a while. I want you here. I have something to tell you about your parents.*

Nathan: *I'll visit tomorrow evening. Are you sure Uncle Lucas won't be home?*

Alma: *I wouldn't lie to you. I'll expect you then.*

Nathan: *I'll be there at six. I have some things I want to get anyway.*

Charles returned to the bedroom as Nathan finished texting Alma.

"I need to visit Alma. She's the woman who raised me after my parents were murdered. My uncle won't be there."

"I'll see that you get there, then. Do you want me there with you?"

"No, I think she wants to talk about my parents' death. I don't know why she waited so long to tell me if she knows something important."

"I understand. You'll find out tomorrow then."

"Are we still going somewhere tonight?" Nathan hoped Charles didn't forget about his marking.

"Are you ready to go to a secret location for your marking now?"

Nathan's face lit up; the thought of finally being marked erasing the stress they had been through.

"Where are we going?"

"It's a surprise. I think you'll like it."

After an hour of driving, Charles parked behind a cabin.

"That's the cabin where we'll stay for the night. We'll get up early for my interview."

"What if I can't deal with my marking?" Nathan bit down on his lip.

"Then you call out your safeword."

"During a marking? If I can't go through with it, does it mean I'm not yours?"

"You're already mine, love. This is just a sign of your submission to me and a reminder who is in charge around here. Remember you have been asking for it. If you've changed your mind about me marking you, then I won't. It won't change anything between us."

"I want it, Sir. It's just I got nervous. I don't want to mess up."

"You'll be fine. Nothing you can't handle."

"You don't have any implements, Sir."

"Who is the Dom?"

"You are, Sir."

Charles carried the suitcase inside, with Nathan slowly following behind him. There was a fireplace with stacked logs beside it. A leather couch and recliners circled the living room. They removed their shoes in the front area. Charles turned on the lights. The TV hung on a wall across from the two recliners. Perfect. Nathan thought it would be nice to move here with Charles.

No one would find them or could bother them when they wanted to spend time alone with each other.

"Take the suitcase in the bedroom, then return."

"Should I take my clothes off?" Nathan asked.

"No. We're going to talk first and have soda."

When Nathan returned, Charles threw logs in the fireplace, lit an old newspaper, then the logs.

"Sit down."

Nathan did exactly what Charles told him, not wanting to make any mistakes on the night of his marking. He was biting down on his lip again. He was nervous and afraid of not being perfect. Charles left him alone in the living room while he went to the kitchen.

A sense of peace overwhelmed him as the flames flickered in various colors. It reminded Nathan of his early childhood and happy days when he was carefree with loving parents. His mother would read him stories and give him hot chocolate with a fire burning in the fireplace before he went to bed. Over the years, Nathan would light a fire in the fireplace on the third floor, make himself hot chocolate, and listen to fairy tales on tape to replicate his childhood when everything was perfect and happy.

Charles returned with two cans of soda. He handed one to Nathan, put the other on the coffee table, then took a seat beside him.

"Do you still want me to mark you?"

"Yes, Sir. It's important to me."

"What does it mean to you?"

"That I'm willing to submit to you at all times in return for your protection and love."

"That makes me very happy to hear you say that. Nathan, are you ready to receive my mark as an outward sign of your obedience to me?" Charles asked.

Nathan's heart skipped with excitement and fear. "Yes, Master Charles."

"Hey, Nathan." Charles smiled when he addressed him at Master Charles.

"Yes, Sir."

"I already love you. I think I fell in love with you on the airplane when I pulled your earplugs out. You had me at that cute little sassy look you gave me."

Charles led Nathan outside behind the house. Large willow trees covered the area as far as he could see. Nathan stopped when Charles stood in front of an old tree.

"Take your clothes off," Charles spoke with confidence and affection.

"Outside, Sir?" Nathan looked around, but thankfully saw no one in sight.

Charles whispered in his ear, "Relax. It's just you and me. Only five of the best. Are you ready?"

"Yes, Sir." Nathan puffed out each word.

Nathan unsnapped his jeans, gently pulling his zipper down with trembling fingers. He pushed his jeans to his ankles and stepped out of them. Nathan's cock was completely hard. His stiff cock head peeked out the top of the elastic waist of his underwear. He pulled them down to his feet and kicked them off, removed his T-shirt, and threw it on the ground. The cool breeze brushed against his backside and private parts.

Charles forced Nathan's hands to wrap around the tree. He tied them together with some rope from his pocket. By now, Nathan dribbled pre-cum down his thighs.

"I'm going to blindfold you, so you won't know what I'm going to do, and you can focus on the marking without distraction. Our relationship is based on trust. Are you okay with that?"

"Yes, Sir. I'm so happy you remembered I like my eyes to be covered."

Charles pulled out a leather blindfold and tied it around Nathan's eyes. "What color are you?"

"Green, Sir."

"Spread your legs."

Nathan allowed his senses to take over, so he missed what Charles said. He kicked them further apart until they were positioned to his liking.

Nathan's rock-hard cock touched the bark, and he didn't like that sensation at all. He heard Charles pull a branch from the tree, and he stripped the leaves away with a pocketknife. *He's making a switch to mark me. It's going to sting.* But once again, the pain/pleasure cocktail mixture enhanced his erection.

"I'm going to give you five strikes with this switch. If it breaks, I'll make another one."

"Thank you, Sir." Nathan would have never thought he'd use a switch from a tree, nor did he ever imagine being marked outside.

"I had to get creative and make this marking personal and special."

"Thank you, Sir."

Charles wielded the switch in the air making a whirling sound. The first strike against his ass stung. He pulled in closer to the tree in hopes of avoiding the strikes, but to no avail. They began from the top of his backside as if Charles was painting red lines with a purpose. The second, third, fourth, and finally, the fifth blow landed on his stinging ass. Each strike hit a little below the previous one. The swats never overlapped on his ass. They stung, but he could deal with it. He belonged to Charles for real now. This felt more formal.

Charles rubbed some cream on Nathan's ass to ease some of the stinging. He heard Charles pull his zipper down, then put a condom on. He spread some lube on the entrance of Nathan's hole. Charles's love and tenderness were all Nathan wanted. Yet, Nathan knew Charles had a bad temper, and when it came out, it freaked him.

Charles licked the back of Nathan's neck. His playing and tickling sent chills through Nathan's body. He bent behind Nathan and allowed his tongue to travel down to his ass. Charles played with Nathan's balls, licking, and sucking. He returned to his entrance and dipped his finger inside. He added two more digits and finger fucked him, shoving his fingers in and out. Nathan moaned with pleasure. When Charles grazed his special spot, he arched his back, needing more, wanting more of Charles.

Nathan's cock stood at full mast. He wanted to scream "Fuck me," but he'd wait for Charles's timing, not wanting to act like he was calling out orders and positions. That was the Dom's job, not Nathan's.

Charles put his hand between Nathan's cock and the tree as he shoved his stiff cock inside. Nathan was grateful for the protection of his cock. The stretch burned, his ass throbbed in pain as Charles slammed in and out, and once again, he banged his prostate. Nathan's cock was oozing precum. He moaned as the burn went away and the pleasure took over.

"You feel so good," Charles panted.

Nathan couldn't answer. Only faint whimpers left his lips. He neared shooting his load. Charles blew his cum into the condom inside him. The constant pounding on his prostate ignited Nathan to shoot spurt after spurt when he finally let himself go.

"You're all mine, now." Charles removed the blindfold and untied the rope.

Nathan nearly collapsed. He slumped to the grass panting, still feeling the aftershocks of his orgasm. Charles threw away his used condom, wiped himself clean, and zipped up his jeans.

"Let's clean up inside, then take a hike," Charles suggested.

"Sounds good, Sir."

"Are you up to it?"

"My ass stings, but I can hike."

They took quick showers separately because the shower was too small for two. They carried a bottle of water with them and hiked for an hour, then returned to get a good night's sleep.

The sound of Charles showering woke Nathan from a deep sleep. His eyes flashed open, and he gasped for air. His ass was stinging again, but he forced himself to sit up slowly, wiping his forehead and neck, both damp with sweat. The air conditioner didn't work very well. He wasn't used to roughing it in heat. He knocked on the bathroom door.

"Come in, love," Charles said.

Nathan let himself into the bathroom. "Good morning, Sir."

Charles slid the shower door ajar. "Good morning. Do you want to go with me when I go for my interview?"

"I'd love to go," Nathan said.

A slow smile worked its way across Charles's face and spread to his eyes. After they showered and played around, they left for the hotel so Charles could change into a suit.

CHAPTER TWENTY-SEVEN

Charles

Charles's phone rang as soon as they arrived at their hotel room. He answered it.

"I'm calling to wish you good luck with your interview. They need someone available right away. They'll hire you on as a substitute, and when it goes through all the hoops, you'll be permanent. Don't worry, you're in."

"Thanks, Dad."

"Also, I found out that Blanken has been under investigation for trafficking teens to Europe. Apparently, I didn't need to send him a message. Word has it, he's left the country to avoid prosecution. No one knows where he is."

"That's excellent news. Thanks. You always come through for me."

"And you have capitalized on the opportunities your mother and I provided. That's the best way to say thank you."

"I can't tell you how much this means to me."

"I heard David moved to Wales six months ago. I don't know what he is doing there."

"Let's hope he doesn't return and come for Nathan."

"He doesn't want Nathan. He did it to get to you because you had the last say in the relationship. Unfortunately, he hurt both of you in the process. Take care of Nathan. Bring him for a visit. I'd like to meet him."

"You'll meet him. Thanks for everything."

He ended the call with his father, then he dressed for the interview. He'd left his suit and shirt at the service desk to be dry cleaned. He was meticulous with his clothes, especially during interviews. He supposed he got that from his father who was a fashionable businessman.

"I have some good news." Charles stood there in his well-fitted Armani slacks as he buttoned his dress shirt, then he put his tie around his neck. The navy tones of his clothing complimented his blue eyes.

"You do?" Nathan helped Charles with his blue stone cuff links.

"Blanken is no longer in the States. He was under investigation, but he managed to leave. No one knows where he is. He's probably back in the Netherlands. So, you don't have to worry about the contract you were conned into." Charles stood before the mirror and fiddled with his tie, so it was exactly how he wanted it.

"That's a big relief, Sir. I mean it. I've had nightmares about what he was going to do to me. Thank you for taking care of me." Nathan hugged Charles.

"Anything for you. No one will ever hurt you like that man did."

"Where is your interview today?"

"It's a surprise."

"You look good. I hope you get the job if that's what you want."

"I'm ready to go."

"Me too."

Charles enjoyed the scenery on the way to the university where Nathan will be attending classes if Charles had anything to do with it. It all seemed unreal with his father sending him here for an interview, which happened to be the same school that had accepted Nathan. Charles wondered who paid for his tuition since he claimed his uncle didn't pay for anything and his job paid too little for him to pay it himself.

He parked in the parking lot and Nathan remained silent. It made Charles wonder if he had ever been to the campus, or he had no opinion one way or another.

The campus had a multitude of housing and dining options both on and off campus. The area covered ten city blocks across the University of Pennsylvania campus. There were hundreds of retail shops, restaurants, and attractions for students and tourists alike. Charles liked it here and hoped Nathan would too.

"What do you think of this university?" Charles asked.

Nathan laughed. "This is where Jacob and I were accepted next semester, but you already knew that."

"If I get the job here or close by, you can attend. Is that something you would want?"

"I would like that and now I want you to get the job. What if you don't get it?"

"Don't worry. I have the job."

"Do you mind if I walk around while you have your interview?"

"That's a great idea." Charles leaned over and kissed Nathan. "Meet me at the Mason Café." He pointed to the nearby cafe. "Give me two hours."

Charles walked into the Administration building and checked in at the desk. They told him to go down the hallway to room 102. He made his way there and walked into a waiting room. He checked in at another desk. They opened the door and directed him into a large room. There was a long table with several men and women waiting for him.

"Sit down, Mr. Moore," a gray-haired man said.

Charles sat down. The man introduced himself as Dr. Higgins, then he introduced the department chair and all the members from the English department. Each told him something they found positive in his resume.

"Your father provided us with your resume. It's quite impressive," Dr. Higgins said.

"Thank you."

"Why did you leave your position as headmaster in London?" Dr. Higgins asked.

"They asked me to leave because they didn't approve of my lifestyle. It was a private school and they can fire people at their whim. They don't follow any norms other than what the rich donors want."

"It is a well-respected private school in London. What exactly was so nefarious in your lifestyle that they asked you to leave?" Dr. Watson asked. She wore her gray hair in a bun on top of her head. She looked like she belonged in a church pew singing hymns rather than asking him ridiculous personal questions.

"I'm bisexual."

Another member quickly jumped in and asked, "Do you want to live on campus or off?"

"Off campus. I plan to purchase a home nearby if I get the position."

"Will you be able to take part in university activities?" Dr. Higgins asked quickly, most likely preventing Dr. Watson from asking any more personal questions.

"Yes, of course."

Dr. Watson jumped in and said, "So does that mean you'll be heading up the new LGBT club?"

Charles shifted in his seat and glanced at Dr. Higgins to let him know he didn't appreciate Dr. Watson's questions.

"Dr. Watson, maybe we could both help with that," Charles said.

"What were the last courses you taught?" Dr. Bukowski asked. He was an older man who was a poet. Charles knew of his work.

"I taught English Composition, World Literature, and a creative writing class."

"Were you full-time?" Dr. Higgins asked.

"Yes."

"Do you mind teaching English Literature and novel writing classes?" Dr. Watson asked.

"Not at all. I'd love to teach those courses. I've missed teaching."

"When can you begin?" Dr. Higgins asked

"Today."

"The job is yours. We need you to begin next week. Do you have any questions?"

"Why is this current position available?" Charles asked.

"Dr. Johnson passed away unexpectedly. That's why we need someone next week for the summer semester. Your schedule and office number are all in this folder. Look it over and see if you have more questions." He passed the thick folder to Charles.

He opened it and reviewed the financial conditions, the benefits, and expectations. He noted his office was in the English building on the third floor. There was a key in an envelope. He read the list of books for each course. He supposed Dr. Johnson had chosen these textbooks, all of which were excellent. He looked up to find them watching his every move. Most of the faculty had been quiet, only three had really interviewed him—Higgins, Watson, and Bukowski.

He signed the contract and passed it across the table.

"Welcome to UPenn."

They all got up and shook his hand. They talked for a while.

After he left the interview, he walked to the English building and climbed the steps to his office. He unlocked the door and looked at the books in there, finding many he had in his own collection. He figured no one had bothered to remove Dr. Johnson's for his family. He'd have to find out what to do with them. He had his own books to add to the shelves. His cell phone rang. He sat down behind the mahogany desk as he answered.

"Hello."

"Charles, this is Ben."

"Ben, I haven't heard from you in a long time. What's going on?"

"I suppose you know by now that David is after you again."

"Why is that?"

"He's bored. He went after me too. He ruined my marriage and family. I don't want to go into the details."

"I lost my position at the academy."

"I heard. Well, I hired two men to tail him."

"And?"

"He's in Wales and is setting up a new location to traffic American teens to Europe. He has this chat room where he picks them up."

"How do you know this?"

"I know some men who used to work for him. They have to be a few steps ahead of him."

"What about the gambling and prostitutes?"

"He's still into that, but his new focus is gay boys in chat rooms. He wants them young."

After talking a while longer, Charles felt nauseous when the call ended.

Charles made numerous phone calls from his office since he had time to spare before he met Nathan for lunch. His father had sent him a list of properties near the university. He had planned to look himself, but his father beat him to it. He certainly was obsessed with getting him moved into the area. Charles still had questions about Dr. Johnson, who suddenly passed away, leaving the perfect job for him. His father had a long reach in Pennsylvania, which concerned him. Would he kill someone to make a position for him? He looked up Dr. Johnson on the internet and found out the man died of a long-term blood disease. A wave of relief swept through him when he realized his father didn't have anything to do with the death. For the most part, his father conducted his business within the law. Years ago, his father had been a member of the Board of Trustees at the University of Pennsylvania, so he received newsletters about university job openings. He had totally forgotten that.

He worried about the subject matter of Alma's conversation with Nathan this evening. Hopefully, she didn't reveal anything shattering his world. His thoughts moved to David again. The man wasn't just deadly; he was seriously unbalanced. Recalling living with him years ago reminded Charles how he'd lived one step away from death on a daily basis. David ruined any trust he had, but it was time for him to put the past behind him.

CHAPTER TWENTY-EIGHT

Nathan

Nathan was waiting for Charles when he arrived at the café. After ordering cheeseburgers and drinks, they found a table outside.

"How was your interview?" Nathan asked.

"I got the job."

"What will you teach?'

"English Literature and some writing courses. I start next week, so we have to move near here so I can work and you'll be nearby for school next semester."

"I hope you're not my English professor."

"Why not?"

"Because we're together."

"I haven't been assigned to any freshman classes, so you and Jacob are safe."

"You look happy about this move."

"I am. I loved my job as headmaster, but some of the people I worked with were too institutionalized and set in their ways. They weren't open to change and improvement. I worked like hell to get them to change things."

"What about your friend James? Are you going to miss him?"

"James is moving back to the States in a couple of months."

"What about Tyler?"

"Tyler will move with him. He'll get him papers so he can stay. He can attend school as an exchange student for up to four years."

"That's good."

As they drove away from the university, Charles spoke up. "I'm going to drop you off to see Alma. Call if you need me."

"I have my own truck and can drive to the hotel."

"I didn't know you had a truck."

"I have a motorcycle too."

"Who paid for them?"

"My uncle. He wanted me to run errands for him." Nathan didn't like Charles asking him so many questions. He acted like he hadn't believed how cruel his uncle was to him when he was growing up. If Alma hadn't been there, he didn't know what would have become of him. Uncle Lucas could have locked him in the barn without food and water. He wouldn't put it past him to let Nathan die a slow, painful death. Uncle Lucas made good use of Nathan's cheap labor—he had taken advantage of Nathan's hard work.

"Did he pay for your tuition?"

"No, but he acts like he did. He took money that was set aside for my college."

"I see."

"Do you think he'll get out of jail?"

"I think he will. With his money and standing, he'll get away with shooting someone on his property." Charles parked the car, letting Nathan out.

"See you tonight," Nathan said.

"Yes. I'll be in the hotel room making arrangements for the move."

"Are we going back?"

"No, I'll have my solicitor take care of everything. James will help too. I have no reason to return. My new teaching position begins next week. Are you going to be okay going in alone?"

"Yes. See you later." Nathan jumped out of the car and walked to the front door.

The old house had given sanity to Nathan when he needed a shelter away from his sorrows. He loved the weatherworn red door and matching shutters. He used to sit on the front porch in a wicker chair listening to the chattering horses. He went to the barn to visit the horses first, stopping to talk to his horse as he brushed her. He missed working with the horses and teaching. After he checked out the others, he left the barn and made his way to the front of the house.

He unlocked the door and went inside. Alma ran down the long hall to meet him. Nathan hugged her, and she teared up. The feeling of comfort and safety overwhelmed Nathan and he realized he should have told her he would be leaving. He had clearly hurt her by disappearing without any explanation.

"Nathan, I'm so happy to see you! I was so worried about you." She stood looking up at him as she was a few inches shorter.

"I'm fine, nothing to worry about." Nathan felt guilty for causing her any worry. She looked thinner than normal. Maybe she hadn't eaten much after he'd left.

"I got up early and went to the butcher for the perfect eye of round roast beef to make your favorite dinner."

He followed her into the large country kitchen. He took his seat as he always did and watched her cook. Uncle Lucas had told Nathan not to help Alma because she was paid to cook. The aroma of the roast cooking reminded Nathan of his birthdays when she had made his favorite dinner. She never disappointed him with her cooking. He never treated her like a hired worker in the home the way Uncle Lucas did. As far as he was concerned, she was family.

"Are you going to tell me where you were?" Alma asked as she mashed the potatoes.

"I went to London to meet a man."

"Did you find what you were looking for?"

"I did, but it wasn't the man I thought I'd be meeting. He never showed up at the airport."

"Why didn't you fly back immediately?"

"I had other problems I had to deal with. I thought it would be best to stay there."

"What have you gotten yourself into?" She turned around looking upset.

"It's handled. No need to worry about me."

"Are you going to be staying here tonight?"

"No, but I'm staying close. I'm going to school next month. Alma, if you haven't figured it out, I'm gay. I have a boyfriend. I'm moving in with him."

"I've known you were gay since you were a child, and your uncle knew a little later than I did. He's not pleased about it, but there wasn't much he could do, so he never confronted you."

"So he knows? Wow! I'm so sick of him and his attitude." He was surprised to hear his uncle had known but didn't say a word about it.

"Is Jacob your boyfriend?"

"No. We're best friends."

"You know Lucas never wanted children, or he would have had them. He raised you the best he could. I tried to step in between when he was unreasonable."

"You really raised me since I was twelve, and I'm grateful you were here. Would you tell me about my parents?" Alma knew how unreasonable Uncle Lucas was only too well, and that was putting it mildly. He was a raging monster if his orders were ignored. Nathan had never understood why Alma stayed on.

"It isn't going to be easy to tell you this. Your parents were your adoptive parents."

"Then why did Uncle Lucas take me in?" Nathan heard what Alma had said about his parents, but he didn't internalize it or try to make any sense of it. They were still his parents and always would be.

"He took you in because your father was his brother. But there is another reason why."

"Why? Don't tell me he's my father because I'll never accept that." Nathan didn't like where this conversation was going. He loved his parents, and now out of the clear blue, they weren't his birth parents. How could that be? They had baby pictures of him when he was born. He didn't remember any other parents but them. They loved him more than anything in the world. That was what both of them had said. They called him their blessing.

"No, he's not your birth father. He took you because I asked him to raise you with me. He agreed if I continued to work for him as his cook and housekeeper."

"Why did you want me?"

"Because I am your birth mother. I was incredibly young at the time, and your Uncle Lucas knew your parents wanted a baby, but they weren't able to have children. Your uncle told me about them, and they adopted you. I thought it was best for your parents to raise you. They were good people and had money to give you opportunities. I had none of that." She sliced the roast beef, set it on a platter and put the mashed potatoes in a bowl along with her homemade brown gravy. She had even baked bread. Everything was on the table. She poured him lemonade from freshly squeezed lemons.

"You had love to give me, and you cared about me my entire life. Aside from my parents, you have loved me more than anyone. You did the right thing. They were the best parents anyone could have wished for. I'll always love them, but you're right up there with them."

"Are you going to ask me who your birth father is?" She sat down at the table and put a napkin on her lap.

"I like the father I had. You never had a boyfriend, so I have no idea." He cut a piece of beef.

"I worked for your uncle as housekeeper and cook. On my vacation, I decided to help the poor in Brazil. That's where I met your father. Things happened. When I returned to work, I told Lucas I was pregnant. That's when he decided it would be best to put you up for adoption at the time of your birth, but then the next day, Lucas said his brother wanted a baby. So, when you were born, you went straight to them, and I sadly returned to work for Lucas."

"Did Uncle Lucas make you give me up or did you want to do that?"

They were finishing up their dinner. She cleared the table and put everything in the dishwasher. Nathan wasn't done with the conversation. He wanted to know more and what part Uncle Lucas had played in her decision. She cut him a piece of strawberry pie topped with whipped cream before she sat back down.

"This is delicious. The entire meal was so good. You treat me like a king."

"Because you are worthy of everything that a king has, and then some."

"Are you going to answer my question about Uncle Lucas?" He licked the whipped cream off his fork.

"That's a tough question. I was only sixteen at the time. He pressured me, but I made the final decision."

"Why were you working full-time as a housekeeper when you were sixteen?" Alma had never discussed her past before, and there had to be a good reason. He knew there had been trouble in the past, and her life was difficult working for his crazy uncle. She stayed here to raise him while she endured daily abuse from Uncle Lucas.

"I ran away from home. It's a long story, but I couldn't stay there anymore. So, Lucas took me in. I've worked for him all these years."

"Tell me about my father." He hoped she never had slept with Lucas. Why would she?

"He was handsome and intelligent like you. He was a doctor from Switzerland. When our charity work ended, he returned home and never contacted me, so he has no idea about you."

"Do you remember his name?" Nathan finished his pie, got up and rinsed the plate and put it into the dishwasher. He took her empty plate and did the same.

"Yes, his name is Dr. Robert le Souter."

"Why are you telling me now?"

"Let's talk in the living room."

CHAPTER TWENTY-NINE

Nathan

They moved to the living room, both sitting on recliners. The room was large with a fireplace and a huge TV. They'd spent many hours in this room watching movies together when Uncle Lucas was working or traveling.

"Lucas would never tell you. He believes in keeping the past buried, especially when it comes to you. He told me never to discuss your parents with anyone, especially you. The reason I needed to tell you now is I was afraid you might disappear again and maybe never come back. When you left, I was heartbroken. I thought I'd lost you all over again."

"I'm sorry I didn't tell you, but I worried you might tell Uncle Lucas. I'll never be out of your life. I know you sacrificed to raise me. You had no life other than this home and me."

"I wouldn't have betrayed you, only tried to talk you out of leaving the country. Where did you meet this man?"

"On the internet. It was a big mistake on my part, but I met another man. He just happened to sit by me on the plane. He was worried about me traveling alone to meet a stranger. You might know him. His name is Charles Moore."

"Isn't he married to one of your high school teachers?" Alma asked.

"He was. He's divorced now."

"And he's interested in you? He's much older." Alma raised her eyebrows.

"He's bisexual and yes he is interested in me." Nathan stood and walked over to Alma. She had light hair and blue eyes like his. How did he not see that he looked a lot like her? No one who knew them both had ever brought that up. Not even Jacob. Did he know about this?

He leaned over Alma and hugged her. "I love you so much. You were my mother for the second part of my life. If it weren't for you, I don't know what would have happened to me."

Alma hugged him as she cried on his shoulder. "I wish I could have kept you and raised you myself, but I didn't have the means to see to all your needs."

"It's okay, Mom. I always wanted to call you mom because for years that was who you were to me."

"We do have a special bond."

"Yes, we do. I'm going to pack some things then I've got to go back to meet Charles. I'm going to take the truck. When we're settled in our new home, I want you to meet him."

"I'd like that. I'm so happy you're going to school. I worried you didn't want to go anymore."

They went upstairs together and began gathering his possessions. He got his laptop and all the other devices he wanted. Alma went to her room and fetched him her large suitcases.

"You can use my suitcases. I hope we still see each other a lot. I'm going to miss you here." Alma had tears in her eyes. She truly was sad he was leaving.

He loved Alma as much as he loved his adoptive parents. Knowing how they had loved him when they had adopted him made him feel even more loved by them. It was so unfair they had to die in such a violent manner. They were truly good people, who should have been blessed with long lives, but someone cut their lives short.

"Thanks. Of course, I will. Are you going to leave your job here?"

"I don't know yet. As you know, your uncle doesn't pay well. I need to look for a job, but I don't have any high-paying skills."

They turned and looked at each other when they heard heavy footsteps coming up the stairs. The door hit the wall when Uncle Lucas barged into his room.

"Where the hell were you?" Uncle Lucas's face was beet red.

"Does it matter? I'm leaving now," Nathan said.

"You will not leave this house without my permission. Do you know I was hauled down to the police station because of your disappearance? You made me look like a fool in town. You work for me, and I didn't give you time off for a vacation across the Atlantic Ocean. I docked your pay for leaving."

"I quit. I returned to clear your name, but I'm not staying here." Somehow, Uncle Lucas had known where he was all this time. He was in no rush for him to return until the police blamed him for his disappearance.

"Did you hear me? You will not leave here. You have work to do."

Alma glowered at Lucas in disbelief. "Lucas, he's going to college and is moving out now."

"Not now. He has another month to work for his tuition. I didn't pay for him to go to school without him working for it."

"How dare you claim to have paid my tuition. My parents set that money aside in a special account for my education. So, I don't owe you anything."

Lucas stormed across the room and shoved Nathan against the wall. "Don't you dare talk to me like that. You owe me your life. I know who you are and what shit you're up to using my name. You're nothing but some whore's bastard, and don't forget it."

"Don't you dare call my mother a whore." Nathan was pinned against the wall, unable to move away.

"Lucas! What's wrong with you?" She had tears rolling down her face.

"I want you out of here, Alma. You put him up to this. I warned you about encouraging his lifestyle."

Her skin paled, but she didn't leave the room.

"But you aren't going anyplace." He pointed to Nathan.

"Go to hell. You're no one to me."

Uncle Lucas punched Nathan in the ribs. Nathan tried to take a deep breath, but his ribcage hurt too much. His head swam in confusion. His stomach tightened and hurt. Then the slapping began.

"Stop hurting him," Alma yelled. She tried to pull him off Nathan, but he shoved her to the floor.

"Leave my mother out of this." Nathan managed to hit Uncle Lucas, but it glanced off his cheek.

"She's not your mother. She's a whore I fuck and nothing more. I don't know what she's filled your head up with, but she's not your mother."

This time, he punched Nathan in the gut. He doubled over, gasping for air.

"You're lying to me," Nathan shouted.

Alma ran out of the room. Why would she leave him now when he needed her? Would he ever see her again? He needed to get away from his uncle. The thought of him fucking his mother turned his stomach. Why did she allow him to do that to her? She wanted to be near him and for this, she had to endure hell on Earth.

"I'm leaving. Get out of my way." Nathan figured he had to leave without his things. He didn't want to fight with his uncle anymore. He couldn't beat a violent, angry monster.

"I'll shoot you first."

"You don't get to tell me what to do. Fuck off."

"If you leave this house, you're a dead man. Alma won't be able to save you from my wrath this time. It's time you pay the price for destroying the Neumann family name."

"I'm leaving without my things." Nathan broke away from Uncle Lucas.

Uncle Lucas tackled him with a clean shoulder-to-shoulder hit, pushing Nathan to his backside on the floor. The next moment, he pointed a handgun at Nathan's head and kicked him. Fear paralyzed his diaphragm. He gasped, doubled over, then curled into a ball, covering his head. Nathan absorbed the trauma, swallowing the humiliation. But the gun frightened him.

"This is your last warning. You won't be moving in with that mobster. He'll bring death upon this house. You're nothing but a faggot."

The pain from Uncle Lucas's hateful words and grave threats dug deeper into him. Did he want him dead because he was gay, or did he want Nathan's share of the money and property? He scanned for a safe path out of the room, but with a gun to his head, he saw no way out.

Within minutes, Charles appeared in the doorway with Alma behind him, unnoticed by his uncle as his attention was on Nathan. A wave of relief washed over him when he realized Alma hadn't abandoned him. She had done the right thing to save him as she often did in the past. How did Charles get here so fast? If she called him, it would have taken longer, but he was here to save him. That is if Uncle Lucas didn't blow his head off first.

"Step away from Nathan, now!" Charles ordered in a firm voice with his hand in his pocket.

"Who let you in here?" Uncle Lucas sent Alma a deathly glare.

"He won't let me leave," Nathan shouted.

"Put the gun away," Charles spoke louder this time.

Ignoring Charles, he spoke to Nathan again. "You will not move in with that Moore mobster." He faced Charles. "Tell him who you really are?"

"What are you talking about? Put that damn gun down before you hurt Nathan." Charles had a gun in his hand, aimed at Uncle Lucas.

"You're part of the Atlantic City crime syndicate. You worked for David Galante for years until your father bailed you out of it. Scum like you don't get to take Nathan."

Nathan understood why Charles never told him about David, but he needed to explain everything to him if they could safely walk out of this room in one piece.

"And you put a hit on your own brother and his wife. I can have you taken out within hours with one phone call to my father, so put the fucking gun away and let Nathan leave with me."

"Is that true? Did you put a hit on my parents?"

"Don't believe that mobster's lies. I bet he never told you he worked for David. He was David's hitman. Did he ever mention he killed for money? I bet he failed to tell you that little tidbit. Now, he wants to turn you against your family."

"Let him leave, or I'll make that phone call to my father."

Uncle Lucas turned to Nathan. "Once you leave this house, you've lost your fifty percent ownership and the money stays with me." He moved his gun from Nathan's head, but still held it in his hand.

"Nathan, leave now," Charles said.

"Are you going to leave with that bastard?" Uncle Lukas asked.

"I'm leaving but I will have someone come for my things," Nathan said as he walked out of the room. Charles and Alma followed behind him.

Once they were outside, Charles said, "Alma, I can put you up in a hotel room."

"No, thank you. I have somewhere to go. Call me when you two are settled."

"I'll wait for you in the car, Nathan." Charles got into his car.

"Why did you let him hurt you like that? You worked for him all these years. Why did you let him fuck you?" Nathan asked.

"I had to be here for you. I was afraid of what he would do if I wasn't here. That's why. I have no love for him. I didn't have any other choices."

Nathan hugged his mother and whispered, "You have choices now. You don't have to stay with him anymore."

"Now you're grown up and have Charles, I won't worry as much."

"Do you think Uncle Lucas was telling the truth about Charles working for the mob?"

"He's no longer involved. He's turned his life around. His father is very influential, and I'm sure he protected him."

"I'll call you when we're settled in. If you need any help, call me." He gave her a long hug then went to the car.

CHAPTER THIRTY

Charles

Charles wanted to keep the conversation in the car light until they got to the hotel room.

"Did Alma call you?"

"Yes, she did, but I was at the front door at the time. She let me in and told me what was going on."

"Why were you there?"

"I had a feeling something was wrong. I couldn't wait for you to come home. I had to make sure you were okay and see you weren't hurt."

"I'm glad you came, but you owe me an explanation about David and what you did for him."

"We'll talk about David when we're in the hotel room. It's not a conversation for the car while I'm driving."

Nathan remained quiet the rest of the trip to the hotel. He stared out of the window, trembling.

Once they were inside the hotel room, Charles noticed a bruise on his face. Not a good sign. His contagious smile had ceased to exist. He looked dog-tired. The shine in his eyes was gone, and his eyes were dazed and distant. He resembled a plastic doll. It was as if Nathan was somewhere else. He removed his shoes as though every movement pained him. The dead silence worried Charles. Something bad had happened before he had gotten there, and he wanted the details.

"Hey, you have a bruise on your face." Charles pulled Nathan into his arms and looked closely at the black and blue mark on his cheek.

"I have an ugly headache."

Charles went through his bag on top of the dresser and found some painkillers. He filled a glass with water and brought them to Nathan. "Take these."

Nathan studied the pills, then washed them down with water.

"Talk to me. What the hell went on before I got there?" Charles closed the drapes and turned out the lights.

"I learned new information about my parents."

"Lie down on the bed. I want you to tell me everything and then I'll tell you about David Galante."

Nathan sat on the bed, leaning back on the headboard. Charles soaked a washcloth in cold water, then put it on Nathan's forehead. "Close your eyes."

Charles didn't quite know how to fix what was wrong with Nathan. He got Nathan a Coke and himself a beer, then sat beside him on the bed.

"Tell me, love." He wanted Nathan to explain the bruise. *Why wouldn't he want me to know?*

"Alma told me my parents adopted me, and she's my birth mother."

"How do you feel about that?" Charles feared Nathan was less than delighted with the news. It was a shock, but that didn't explain the mark on his face. His uncle had hit him hard enough to bruise. He needed to know what happened before he arrived there.

"I'm not upset Alma's my birth mother. I love her as much as I loved my parents. She told me the story of how and why she had to give me away. She was only sixteen at the time, working for my uncle, who used her as his sex toy. He made her give me up to his brother. She said she couldn't take care of me. I'm upset she gave up her entire life to raise me. She endured abuse on a daily basis. That makes me upset and depressed. I was the cause of her sad life."

"We can put her into a condo."

"We will have to convince her, but I think we can. My uncle called her a whore, and he called me a whore's bastard."

Charles didn't like the direction this story was moving. That would explain the bruise.

"He showed up after dinner while I was upstairs packing. He punched, slapped, and kicked me because I wanted to move out." Nathan removed his jeans to show Charles his bruises.

"If I had known he was going to be there, I would have gone with you." Charles took Nathan in his arms. "I'm so sorry he hurt you."

"I guess they let him out early. Alma wasn't sure when he'd be out. He didn't call to let her know."

"Why did your uncle hurt you? Were you fighting before I got there?"

"He wouldn't let me leave. I was packing, and he told me I owed him money for my college tuition, so I couldn't leave. I had to work until school begins."

"I'm so sorry you had to deal with him."

"He said you worked for David Galante, and you were his hitman. Were you?"

"I worked for David Galante for two years when I was a teenager. I went through a rebellious patch and left home to live with him. I did some things I'm not proud of. When the relationship turned violent between us, I called my father and asked for help."

"Were you his hitman?"

"As I said, I did things I'm not proud of, but I never killed a man."

"Was he your boyfriend?"

Charles nodded. "David was much older than I was, and he convinced me my life would be better if I left home. I was young and stupid when I left home for him. I didn't know what he and his mob family were into. He had me doing things I'll never forgive myself for."

"Is David Galante the man who conned me in the chat room?"

"Yes. That's why I didn't want you to know about him. I was only seventeen when I was with him. My father had a big reach on the East Coast. He saved me from those thugs. They threatened to torture me if I left the family. My father helped me return to school. Then, later on, I got married. My father made sure I was safe, and he still does."

"What did you do to David to make him hate you so much?"

"I left him. No one leaves David and lives to talk about it. He was obsessed with me. When my father took me out of there, he threatened he'd destroy every relationship I had. I just recently found out that he was responsible for ruining my job in London. He also deliberately created stories, so Hans would leave me. He actually did me a favor on that one, but I didn't want Hans hurt in the process. Hans was damaged by David's lies. He used you to get back at me, too. I still don't understand how you got into the mix with us. But he was the one using my name in the chat room. Maybe he was looking for another boy, but he didn't show up for you. I still don't know why he didn't pick you up, but be thankful he didn't."

"I wish I could tell him off for hurting and using us."

"He's dangerous, deadly dangerous. You wouldn't know that by looking at him. He's a good-looking man. That's one of the ways he ropes you in. But the odd thing is you never saw him, and you still bought into his con. He's the king of seduction."

"I know I made a mess by believing his lies. He said all the things I wanted to hear, but he didn't mean any of them."

"That's exactly how he conned me too. I didn't want you to go through what I did. I wasn't sure it was David until I talked to a friend who had similar experiences with him."

"It's because of him we met, you know."

"I love you, pretty boy. Our meeting was life-changing."

"I love you, too."

"I want to make love to you. No spanking. Just pure loving."

"When?" The sweetest smile crawled across his face.

"Later. I found five properties I want you to look at." He fiddled with his phone and handed it to Nathan. "Take your time and check out the places, then tell me which one you want to live in with me."

Nathan remained quiet as he went through the photos of each home. "I like this one the best."

"That's the same one I liked the best, too. We'll put in a bid on it tomorrow."

"Are we really going to live happily ever after?"

"Let's get a head start now."

THE END

ABOUT THE AUTHOR

I am from Huntington Beach, Ca. I taught various subjects at a Continuation High School in Los Angeles, California for 27 years. I obtained a Bachelor's of Arts Degree in History, Secondary Social Science Credential and a Master's Degree in Secondary Reading and Secondary Education from California State University, Long Beach. I also enrolled in some creative writing classes at UCLA.

CONNECT WITH BRINA BRADY

I would love to hear from my readers, so please drop me a line.

My email address:

mailto:brinabrady@gmail.com

Please visit my WordPress Blog here:

http://brinabrady.wordpress.com

Friend me on Facebook here:

https://www.facebook.com/brina.brady.3

Follow me on Twitter here:

https://twitter.com/BrinaBrady

Follow me on BookBub here:

https://www.bookbub.com/authors/brina-brady

Follow me on Pinterest here:

http://www.pinterest.com/brinabrady/

Join my Reader's Group here:

https://www.facebook.com/groups/146904702344189/

Follow me on Instagram:

https://www.instagram.com/bradybrina/

Sign up for my newsletter:

http://brinabrady.bravehost.com/Newspaper/

OTHER BOOKS

RENT ME SERIES 1-5

Rent Me (Book 1)

Russian mobster spanks his rent boy. Ouch!

Rent Boy Brennen wants to belong to his lover Dmitri Dubrovsky. The Russian mobster controls every inch of his life in and out of bed. Brennen works for Dmitri's escort service. His only desire is to please his lover. When Dmitri marries Nika, his lover moves him out of their home to an apartment in Beverly Hills and tells him nothing has changed.

What is Brennen going to do now?

Brennen does not understand his lover's Russian culture not allowing homosexuality. Two different cultures and age difference clash.

Own Me (Book 2)

Make Me (Book 3)

For Me (Book 4)

Find Me (Book 5)

BEND OVER SERIES 1-4

Bend Over (Book 1)

Runaway 18-year-old Shane O'Rourke is living under the Huntington Beach Pier.

He carries many secrets from his past. Shane wasn't allowed to explore his sexuality when he lived home with his father, The Reverend. His submissive nature and desires had to remain fantasies.

Shane meets a dark stranger on the beach. Julien Callier is a Dom from Martinique and is sixteen years older than Shane. Bad boy Shane wants to win the heart of Julien Callier and become his sub. But does he really understand what Julien expects from his boy?

Julien's heart goes out to this gorgeous boy, and he takes him under his wing, grooming him to be his sub. Julien is determined to let Shane experience the good life, even financing his education, but he's challenged at every turn by Shane's rebellious nature.

When Shane's defiant behavior threatens to come between them for good, Julien has to act fast to teach Shane the meaning of real submission.

Can Julien tame the bad boy? Can Shane give up his old ways of stealing, lying, and using drugs? The playroom is open.

Don't Throw Me Away (Book 2)

Spanked in the Woodshed (Book 3)

Breaking Roadblocks (Book 4)

THE IRISH RUNAWAY SERIES 1-3

The Runaway Gypsy Boy (Book 1)

Twenty-year-old Daniel Serban loses his dancing job and threats of being outed to his family force him to flee Limerick, Ireland. Daniel fears his father and the other gypsy men will force him to marry his betrothed or bring bodily harm to him for being gay.

As chance would have it, he ends up in Cleary's Pub, a gay leather bar in Galway where he meets the grouchy, ginger-bear Ronan O'Riley. Daniel had no idea how much meeting the Dom would transform his life.

Ronan O'Riley has been unable to move on since the death of his sub a year ago, that is

until a troubled gypsy boy steps into Cleary's. Ronan's lonely existence is about to change.

Can Ronan convince Daniel to trust him or will Daniel's fears of his past ruin any chance of a relationship? Unexpected, heated attraction in the barn ignites their relationship to move forward. Though the two men have many of the same dreams, Daniel's secrets, and Ronan's need to gain Daniel's trust are just a few of the many challenges they must overcome if they are to be together.

MASTER CLEARY'S BOYS (Book 2)

Master Braden's Houseboy (Book 3)

BURIED SECRETS SERIES

Buried Secrets (Book 1)

When Alek Belanov loses his family at four years old, his Russian mobster uncle raises him.

Now, at twenty-two, Alek wants nothing more than to find out who murdered his family and why. After Alek gets out of prison for a crime he didn't commit, his uncle sends him away to the Gay Protection Society, claiming Alek's life is in danger.

Sexy Rafe Escobar is the head of the secret Gay Protection Society, and he chooses Alek as his personal charge. Rafe warns Alek that if he breaks security rules, he will discipline him. Alek has some slip-ups here and there, but he adores his protector and wishes to please him in every way.

Alek quickly finds his place among the other men who seek shelter and those who guard them. What was supposed to be a safe haven becomes a group on the run as security breaches and threats force them to move from town to town.

Is Rafe and Alek's relationship strong enough to withstand the secrets and deceptions of people trying to destroy them?

Taming Emilio (Book 2)

Dante's Discipline (Book 3)

Gang member Dante Medina committed an unforgivable offence against his family, friends, and gang. It was only a matter of time until his homeboys would jump him out of the gang or worse. His life in East Los Angeles as he knew it would end at the age of twenty-four.

His father sent his two older brothers to take him to his aunt's house in Santa Monica. Dante thought his family was working together to save him from the gang, but that wasn't what happened.

Ex-army officer, protector and Dom, James chose to protect Dante. He is warned to never break the security rules and to accept James's decisions at all times, or his punishment will be harsh. Dante happily accepted the rules and consequences of the Gay Protection Society conditions.

Unfortunately, no amount of protection can alter the gang's determination to take Dante down for good.

MOBSTERS' GAY SONS SERIES

Without Respect (Book 1)

Blurb

An Italian mobster raises three sons, but Sal's youngest son, Benito Banetti, is gay. His father would never permit Ben to be in an openly gay relationship. But Ben intends to change that when he finds the man he wants. When it turns out the man Ben's been seeing is a Banetti family enemy, his father gives him an ultimatum. Either he marries his cousin and all is forgotten, or if he chooses to be with Mishka Chernov, a Russian mobster, he will disown him.

Mishka Chernov took over his family's business out of love and respect for his father; however, he has come to realize he isn't suitable for this top position in the family. Mishka meets a beautiful man at a sleazy bar, and when he finds out who this man is, he still wants him regardless of the problems Ben Banetti would cause his family's business. Mishka wants the same freedom and separation from family business that Ben has.

Without Respect is about two men raised by mob bosses, realizing their families are enemies, but neither is willing to walk away. This story is book one of a MM romance that follows their relationship. It has some D/s and light BDSM elements.

Loyalty Required (Book 2)

Family Ties (Book3)

STANDALONES

Cabin Commotion

Playboy Blaze is the son of Sal Bossio, a New York City Italian mobster. His father orders him to his Vermont cabin for one month while he settles mob business. Blaze hires a rent boy for one month, but unexpected events occur, and he finds himself alone in Vermont. When he reaches his cabin, he finds a stranger sleeping in his bed. The gorgeous gingered-haired man could be a hitman sent by his father's enemies.

High-paid escort Marcus graduates college and he's ready to leave The Manor. Working for pimp Kalepo for four years, Marcus believes there's no way out without paying a fatal price. Marcus leaves California on a train to New York City and a bus to a rented Vermont cabin for one month to hide from Kalepo.

Two lonely men solve the cabin commotion by sharing the only bed in the cabin during their sex fest saving hidden pasts and tough decisions until the month ends.

Sir Ethan's Contract

Rich, intelligent, and ridiculously sexy, Sir Ethan finds his submissive left him, breaking their D/s contract. Not wanting to be alone, Sir Ethan places an ad, offering a large sum of money for a submissive man. He wants to take care of a submissive, make rules, and dish out the consequences.

American born Adrien Dubois loses his family when ICE deports them to France. He hooks up with a mean ex-felon in a dilapidated trailer. When Stone abandons him, Adrien finds an ad for a submissive.

Sir Ethan is going to be Adrien's Dominant for one month, and he'll make lots of money. What could go wrong? He's going to take care of Adrien, and all he has to do is follow Sir Ethan's rules or his Dominant will spank him. Adrien is terrified to admit it, deep down he knows that soon he'll beg Sir Ethan to strip him bare and teach Adrien what happens to bad boys.

Two men dumped not looking for love, one needs money, and the other wants convenient sex.

Leather Paddles

He's had it with Doms. Never again...but maybe this one is different.

Twenty-two-year-old Jesse finds himself abandoned by his abusive Dom after four years in an unhappy BDSM relationship. Devastated, he moves in with his best friend, Charlie, and his Dom. He attends college and works in the university library. He doesn't have time nor plans to look for another Dom.

Master Andrew, the owner of BDSM club Leather Paddles, lost his husband five years ago. Ever since, he plays with different subs and is perfectly happy to leave it with that. He doesn't want another boy to call his own.

Once Master Andrew meets Jesse, things click for both of them, but Jesse remains skittish about getting involved with anyone. However, Master Andrew comes up with a plan to rein Jesse in his playroom and his heart.

Other people keep interfering, trying to separate the couple. Are Master Andrew and Jesse up to the challenge to move forward to their happily ever after?

Leather Paddles is a stand-alone MM romance featuring an insecure boy and a strict but caring Master. It has BDSM elements and a guaranteed HEA.

Baby Bear

Abel's heartbreaking childhood contributes to his emotional baggage; his life has been one of hate, denial, and secrecy. His father, a polygamist cult leader, sends young men away from the compound in Utah so at eighteen, his mother drives him to the city. A dancing job opportunity finds Abel moving to Minnesota. Two years later he's mysteriously fired. Without savings, Abel needs a Daddy to take care of him, and he's found the perfect one at the Blue Diamond Diner.

Diner owner Darius Eriksen's dream is to find a boy who needs a Papa Bear to take care of his needs. Darius belongs to the Bearded Papa Bears. Membership requires Papa Bears wanting to be a daddy to a boy; they pledge to love, care, and discipline their Baby Bear. Two years after Darius's Baby Bear leaves him for another Papa Bear, he's ready to find a new Baby Bear and commit again.

HOUSE ARREST WITHOUT a Home

Shawn O'Brien

Pre-law student Shawn O'Brien loses his mind when he finds his live-in boyfriend Jasper Logan with a younger man in their bed. Shawn breaks the law and ends up in big trouble, in danger of losing his scholarship and freedom. He needs a new place to live to serve his house arrest sentence or he will go to jail for six months.

NOAH BRAUN

Successful, District Prosecuting Attorney, Noah Braun has it all: money, friends, and a top career, but he's at risk of losing it all as he grieves the loss of his husband. His father, Judge Braun finds the perfect lover to save his son. The judge asks Noah to take Shawn into his home to complete his sentence.

EVERYTHING CHANGES when Noah and Shawn meet and find themselves living together. Noah is determined to do whatever it takes to prove to Shawn that their relationship will be different from his nightmarish one with Jasper.

Can Noah find a way to win Shawn's heart forever, or will Shawn move on when his house arrest is complete?

Steamy, Age Gap, Hurt and Comfort, Contemporary, Forced Proximity, Destined to Be Together